RECONNECTING IN WILLOW HEIGHTS

WILLOW HEIGHTS SERIES BOOK SEVEN

ABIGAIL BECK

CHAPTER 1

Mary Elle was in the kitchen making breakfast when Michael came down the stairs. Her day shined just a little brighter whenever he was around. Maybe it was a little selfish of her, but she wasn't ready for him to return to California. If it were up to her, he would never go back.

"Good morning, my handsome boy," she said as he came over to give her a good morning kiss on the cheek.

Michael gave Wyatt a nod and sat next to him on the kitchen island. Wyatt held a fist for him, and they bumped fists while sitting side by side. Michael had only been in Willow Heights for two weeks now, but Mary Elle was happy to see that her boys were bonding.

At Wyatt's request, Michael had gone to the park to watch Wyatt play basketball with friends and give him pointers on his technique. Michael had played basketball during High School, and Wyatt loved having an older brother around.

Mary Elle had been worried that Michael would get annoyed having Wyatt hang around him all the time because he was so needy for male role models. Michael seemed to love spending time with him.

Mary Elle placed a plate of food in front of Michael with a stack of pancakes, scrambled eggs, and bacon.

"Eat," Mary Elle instructed as she pushed the plate a little closer.

"May I have some more pancakes, please?" Wyatt asked, holding his plate out for Mary Elle.

"Of course, honey," Mary Elle said as she placed another small stack of pancakes on his plate. This was his third stack; the boy's stomach was like an endless pit.

Mary Elle grabbed the pancake syrup and held it out of his reach before he could get to it.

"Let me," she said as she poured a little over his pancakes.

Wyatt pouted as she did that. He loved drenching his pancakes with syrup, but all that sugar wasn't good for him.

"Good morning, everyone," Thomas said as he entered the kitchen from the side door.

Wyatt and Michael gave him a nod, their mouths too full to talk. Mary Elle gave Thomas a quick kiss. She didn't know how Michael felt about seeing her with Thomas. She knew he approved of her relationship and that he liked Thomas, but who wanted to see their parent kissing someone?

Thomas had been working outside all morning. Even on the weekends, the man didn't know how to stop and just relax. He wasn't one to sit around watching tv all day or leisurely drink a cup of coffee while reading the morning paper. Mary Elle wished he would take some time to relax. He needed to slow down and enjoy life a little more.

"Are you hungry?" Mary Elle asked him.

"No, thank you," Thomas said before sneezing into his handkerchief.

"I can make you some tea, and you should probably drink some meds and get some rest," Mary Elle told him.

Thomas had a cold, but instead of turning into a big baby as most men did, he said he'd rather sweat the cold off. Mary Elle wanted him to stay home and eat soup and rest, but he refused. Thomas didn't really like being taken care of; Mary Elle figured it was because he was used to fending for himself during most of his adult life. She respected his wishes, but that didn't stop her from still trying. She was already starting on her special homemade chicken noodle soup recipe. The secret to getting rid of a cold quickly was with a hearty broth base with many nutrients. At least that's what her mother and grandmother always told her growing up. So far, their logic had never stirred her wrong.

"I'm okay. I'll be going to the stables in a little while," Thomas squeezed her shoulder and said, "I have a lot to do still."

He grabbed a few things around the house and returned to work.

"Any plans for today?" Mary Elle asked the boys.

"I'm going to the sanctuary to help David clean the barn. I've almost saved up enough money for Rosie's birthday gift," Wyatt said as he wiped his face.

Wyatt had taken a second part-time job at the Animal Sanctuary for the summer. Rosie was his new girlfriend, and they seemed to get very serious rather quickly. Mary Elle and Thomas weren't sure how they felt about Wyatt getting so serious about a girl at such a young age, but they knew he was a good kid, and they had to trust him to make his own decisions in life.

"What are you getting her?"

"A necklace and earrings from Rita's store. We passed by her shop the other day, and she really liked them," Wyatt said.

"That's so sweet. I'm sure Rita will give you a great price on them," Mary Elle told him.

"I don't want to ask for a discount. I value her work and want to support her," Wyatt said.

His sentiments touched Mary Elle. Wyatt was such a sweet and thoughtful boy.

"You're such a good boy, and you will be an even greater man. You make me proud every day," Mary Elle said as she placed a hand on his cheek.

"Thanks, Mary Elle. I got to go; I'm going to be late to work," Wyatt said as he jumped off the stool, kissed Mary Elle goodbye, and waved at Michael. He was out the door in no time.

Mary Elle watched him go and thought of how far along he had come since they adopted him. Wyatt had always been a smart, hardworking kid, but he was doing much better now that he was in a stable home and his biological mother was back. He had improved his grades a lot. His spirits were high, and his relationship with his mother improved daily. His mother, Lorraine, had stuck around and seemed to be in a much better place.

It hadn't taken Mary Elle very long to grow a soft spot for her. Once she saw Lorraine was serious about making positive changes in her life, she took her in rather quickly. She and Thomas found a tutor to help Lorraine prepare for her GED test. At first, Mary Elle and Wyatt had accompanied her to the library for her tutoring sessions, but once Lorraine felt more comfortable and didn't need their support, she began going alone. In a week, she'd be taking her GED test and then applying for the local college in Winding Creek once she passed.

"Do you have plans for today?" Michael asked, cutting into Mary Elle's thoughts.

He'd been so quiet that she'd forgotten he was there.

"Well, I have a wedding today at Willow Acres, then I'm

meeting your sisters for dinner. It's a charity auction event. You should join us; they'd love to spend time with you."

"I don't know..." Michael said.

Michael hadn't been spending much time with his sisters since he got here. Mary Elle almost felt he was avoiding them, and she couldn't understand why.

"How are you feeling?" Mary Elle asked.

"I'm fine, mom. Don't worry about me. I did one dumb mistake, and I learned my lesson," Michael said.

Mary Elle could tell he was getting irritated. A lot irritated him lately.

"I'm not here to lecture you or make you feel bad. I just worry about you, Mikey."

"I'm fine, mom."

"Did you ever hear from Samantha again after your sister's wedding?" she asked gently.

She hadn't brought Samantha up since Michael got here, but she had to know what was going on with him.

"No," Michael said, immediately tensing up.

"Did you really love her?" Mary Elle asked.

She had only met Samantha a couple of times, and she'd never liked or understood Michael's relationship with her. They didn't seem happy and in love as newly engaged couples usually did. Mary Elle could never wrap her mind around their relationship.

"No," Michael said, eyes darting all over the room but never meeting his mothers.

"Then why did you ask her to marry you?" Mary Elle asked, more confused now than ever.

"Because I don't deserve the one I love, mom. Isn't that life? We always want what we can't have, and life cruelly throws it in our face every chance it gets," Michael said bitterly.

"What are you talking about, Michael? Why wouldn't you deserve the one you love?" Mary Elle asked.

She had to take advantage because they were alone, and he was finally opening up, but she didn't want to push too hard. Michael never talked to her or anyone about his feelings. He always kept everything bottled up.

"I knew dad was cheating on you when I was in middle school, mom. I saw how sad you were, and I said nothing. Dad made me promise not to. He said he was a man and had needs. He said that it was normal. If I would've been a better person, I would've told you. Instead, I covered for him. I'm so sorry, mom..."

"Oh, honey," Mary Elle said, pulling him into a hug.

She wished she had known about this before. She wished she could've done something to fix this. Bill should've never placed Michael in this position. Mary Elle was so angry right now. She had never felt so much anger towards Bill as she did right now. How could they have failed their kids so badly? Her daughters were finally in a good place now, but she couldn't help but think that if she had spoken up if she would've left Bill, none of her kids would have the trust issues they have now. If only she could've been stronger. If only she could've been a better mother.

CHAPTER 2

"Are you sure you're up for this?" Ruby asked Melanie as she gathered her hair away from her face.

Melanie was having a hard time with morning sickness. She thought this time it would differ from what it had been with Ryder. Unfortunately, this baby didn't want to make it easy on her.

"Yes, I'll just have some ginger tea, and I'll be better in no time," Melanie said as she straightened herself out and brushed her teeth.

She didn't know how she would make it through the day. She had a wedding to photograph this afternoon. Afterward, they went to Winding Creek with Mary Elle, Sienna, and Tiffany. Doctor Banks was hosting a charity event at the Winding Creek Ranch. The theme was high tea. Melanie studied herself in the mirror. She loved being pregnant.

Even with dealing with the morning sickness, she wouldn't change a thing. When she was pregnant, she felt the most beautiful and happy, but she couldn't explain why. She ran a hand down her small bump and straightened her floral stress. She turned to Ruby and found her friend looking down at her hand, which now displayed her beautiful diamond engagement ring with a frown on her face.

"Are you okay?" Melanie asked Ruby.

"Yes, I'm great," Ruby said, flashing her a smile.

Melanie noticed the smile didn't meet her eyes. She'd also noticed that Ruby hadn't been as excited about her engagement as she should've been. Did it have anything to do with Michael? The girls had said nothing to Ruby about the messages Tiffany saw on her phone. They didn't know how to bring it up to her without coming clean about Tiffany snooping and invading her privacy.

"My mom says she convinced Michael to join us," Melanie said as she looked out for a reaction from Ruby.

"That's good," Ruby said, showing no change in emotion.

Melanie expected some kind of reaction. She expected to get a clue from Ruby, but there was nothing. She kept her face completely straight.

"Is Axl coming?" Melanie asked. Maybe this would work.

Axl was Ruby's fiancé. He showed up last week and surprised Ruby by proposing to her. He left the same day he came because he had to travel for work.

"No, he's not back yet," Ruby said.

"Better for us. We get to keep you around longer," Melanie said as she wrapped an arm around Ruby's waist.

Melanie loved Ruby, and she loved the idea of having Ruby as a sister-in-law someday. She never voiced her opinions out loud, though. Ruby never said anything about her feelings for Michael, and Melanie didn't want to make her feel uncomfortable. Also, Tiffany always had a fit at the mere thought of her brother and Ruby dating.

The doorbell rang, and the girls hurried over to see who it might be.

"Welcome!" Melanie said as she opened the door to find

Mary Elle and Michael standing on her front porch.

"You're glowing!" Mary Elle said as she hugged and kissed Melanie.

"Nice to see you again," Melanie said to Michael.

"I'm here now," Michael said as he hugged her.

As they pulled apart, Melanie searched the room for Ruby, but she was nowhere to be found. She hated how weird Michael and Ruby were being around each other. She just wanted everything to go back to the way things were. Why couldn't they just admit their feelings for each other and get it over with?

"I love your outfit," Melanie said to Mary Elle.

Mary Elle struck a pose and blew her a kiss. She wore a faux wrap floral dress, a hat, and espadrille wedge sandals. They wouldn't have much time between events, so they all wore their outfits for the Charity event to leave Willow Acres together after the wedding.

"Tiffany and David won't be at Willow Acres, but they are meeting us at the event. We should get going," Ruby said as she emerged with Ryder in her arms.

Ruby looked at everyone in the room but Michael. Melanie turned to him and felt a pull on her heart once she caught sight of the look on his face.

The siblings had all been very close growing up, but since they were the oldest, Michael and Melanie had always shared a special bond. Growing up, Michael was everything to Melanie. Whenever she had nightmares, he would come into her room and gently wake her. He would then read her favorite books to her until she fell asleep. Michael spent many nights sleeping on the floor next to her bed. He taught her how to ride a bike and how to rollerblade. He did things their father should've done, but he was never around. Michael was always there when she needed him, and now she would be there for him.

* * *

RUBY STOOD BACK and admired all the hard work the team had done to pull off yet another beautiful wedding. She watched as the newly married couple took to the dance floor and whispered promises of forever to each other. She felt a tear stream down her face as she watched them.

Ruby always wanted to experience that type of love. She wanted to know what it was like to have someone be so completely yours. Someone that protected you and only wanted what was best for you. She thought she had that with Michael, but apparently, she'd only been a fool to fall for his charm.

She still couldn't wrap her head around where things had gone wrong between them. Growing up, Michael was always there for her. He was like family to her, just like his sisters and mother. She couldn't imagine a life where any of them weren't in it.

Ruby remembered crying to Michael when Peter Miller told her he wouldn't be going to the school dance with her anymore because he had found a hotter date. Michael had stepped in and taken her. They'd had a wonderful time and even shared a sweet kiss at the night's end. They kept it a secret from their families because they didn't know how anyone would react. Therefore, they decided to remain just friends. But that night was the night that Ruby used to measure every single one of her future dates. No one had ever made her feel as special as Michael had during that High School dance.

Fast forward to almost a year ago when Ruby flew to California for a job interview. She didn't get the job, but while in California, she and Michael reconnected. He took her to all his favorite places all over California, and for the first time in a long time, they let each other enjoy each other 's company without caring about who might see them or what they might think. The chemistry between them was tangible. Ruby had a hard time returning to Atlanta. She didn't know what would happen between them once she left California.

Not being able to stay away from her for too long, Michael surprised her by flying to Atlanta. During this trip, they determined they would date privately before getting their families involved. Things were perfect between them. Although they were in a long-distance relationship, they were sure that there was no one else they'd rather be with than with each other. When Mary Elle invited them to Willow Heights for the camping trip, they knew it would be the perfect time to tell them about their relationship. They'd been going steady for months, which was only the most logical step. They were still crazy about each other and were even discussing marriage.

But Michael changed his mind during that trip. He said he didn't want to take the attention away from Mary Elle and Thomas. Then, two days after the camping trip, he broke up with her out of the blue. He said he didn't deserve her and wanted her to be happy. Only to get engaged to Samantha shortly thereafter.

"Are you okay?" Bailey asked Ruby as she approached her with Lisa.

"Yes, everything is fine. Weddings just make me emotional," Ruby said as she blinked a few tears away.

Ruby hadn't spent much time with Bailey or Lisa, but she remembered them from the camping trip and Melanie's wedding and baby shower. They seemed nice, and Melanie spoke highly of them.

"I don't understand weddings," Lisa said, crossing her arms. "Why spend so much money on something that should be intimate and private? If I ever got married, I would just elope."

"I want a big wedding. I want it all!" Bailey said with stars in her eyes.

"Didn't you just get engaged?" Lisa asked Ruby.

"Yes," Ruby said and held her ring finger hand out for them to see.

The girls oohed and Ahed over the ring.

"Are you having a big wedding or eloping?" Bailey asked.

"I don't know yet. My fiancé is very busy and we've barely discussed the wedding since he proposed," Ruby said, hoping that didn't sound pathetic.

She was having a hard time sounding excited about the wedding and finding it harder to even get motivated to think about it. She usually got a funny feeling in her stomach when she thought about the wedding and it wasn't a good feeling at all. It killed her inside because she knew it wasn't fair to Axl. She met him on a whim and agreed to go on a date with him to get her mind off of Michael. Axl was great. He was older than her and knew what he wanted. He wanted to get married and start a family. What woman wouldn't want that?

"Oh, he's cute," Lisa said, bringing Ruby back to reality.

Ruby followed her gaze, and her eyes landed on Michael. He was watching them, too. When their eyes locked, Ruby couldn't help but scowl at him. She hated the way he made her feel.

"I thought you and Michael were dating for the longest time," Bailey said.

"Yeah, me too! I was so surprised when Melanie told me he was engaged to that woman he brought for the Christmas party," Lisa said.

"Michael and I are just friends. He's single now, so if any of you are interested..." Ruby said before excusing herself.

CHAPTER 3

"You came!" Tiffany said as she pulled her brother into a big hug.

She had seen little of him since he got here from California. The only time she got to see him was when she visited her mother's house.

"Mom made me," he said as he returned the hug.

"I'm happy you came. I've missed you," Tiffany said, squeezing him tighter.

A server passed by with a tea tray, and they each took one, except for Michael.

"Is there a bar?" he asked the server.

"Yes, there's an open bar over there," the server replied, pointing towards the bar.

Michael excused himself and went to get a drink.

"Have you seen the tables? Everything is so cute!" Tiffany said to the others.

There were flowers everywhere, and life-size floral arrangements adorned the room. The tables had tiers of small sandwiches, biscuits, and sweets.

"They really outdid themselves. I should take notes," Mary Elle said with a small laugh.

"I think Patty made the floral arrangements," Melanie said.

Patricia and Dean had broken up a few weeks ago. Working together had been too much for her, and she was now working at Winding Creek Ranch. It hadn't been easy for the team to see her go; she had been a part of their small work family for five years.

"I wonder if she'll be here tonight. I miss her," Mary Elle said.

"Mary Elle! It's so good to see you," Beatrice, the owner of Winding Creek Ranch, said.

"It's good to be here. The place is breathtaking," Mary Elle said as she looked around the venue.

"We've had to step up our game after Willow Acres took you in," Beatrice said, giving her a wink, before heading off to greet other guests.

The group found their table where Rita, Bob, Sienna, David, and Michael were already sitting. Tiffany took a seat in between Michael and David. Ruby sat on the other side of Michael, followed by Melanie and Cade on the other side of her.

"What are you bidding on?" Michael asked, leaning into Tiffany.

She caught a whiff of liquor on his breath and noticed the empty glasses he had already downed. Michael had never been a drinker until now.

"I don't know yet. Has anything caught your eye?" Tiffany answered him.

"Not yet," Michael said before standing. "I'm going to get a drink. Do you want anything?"

"Don't you think you've had enough?" Ruby asked, placing a hand on his forearm.

Michael looked down at the hand Ruby had placed on his arm.

"Careful, Ruby. We wouldn't want anyone thinking you care about me, would we?" Michael said with a sad smile.

Tiffany let out a small gasp and looked at Melanie. Their brother's comment also took Melanie by surprise. What in the world was going on between Ruby and Michael? She looked to the other side of the table, but no one else seemed to have heard his comment. Tiffany turned to Ruby and found her staring down at her lap.

"Is everything alright?" Tiffany asked Ruby in a hushed tone.

"Yes, it's nothing," Ruby replied without meeting her eye.

* * *

MICHAEL REGRETTED his comment as soon as it came out of his mouth. No matter what he did lately, everything always went wrong. He couldn't catch a break, and he knew it was no one's fault but his own. He had ruined everything, and there was no going back now. Even if he could, he knew Ruby was better off without him. He would only break her heart, and he couldn't let himself do that.

"Michael, please stop. Pace yourself. I know you want to have a good time and forget things that you're clearly not ready to talk about, but you're acting reckless," Melanie said, coming up behind him.

"Mel, you don't understand. I'm not perfect like you and Tiff. I'm not good. Apparently, I'm not good enough for anyone to love," Michael said as he took a seat at a different table and took a sip of his gin and tonic. He sounded pathetic, but he didn't care. It was the truth.

He deserved all the bad things that life threw at him. He'd hurt enough people in his lifetime.

"Don't say that. We all love you. You are more than enough; you just don't see how important and special you are to us. Don't keep yourself from being happy by hiding behind liquor in a drunken stupor," Melanie said as she sat next to him.

Michael loved his sisters, and he knew they only wanted the best for him, but when were they going to understand he wasn't the person they thought he was. They held him up with so much regard, but he would only let them down. He was just like their father, and he always would be.

"Thanks, Mel. I wish it were that simple, but you don't know everything I've done. I don't deserve happiness."

Would Melanie still be standing here saying this to him if she knew it was his fault their mother had got her heart broken? Would she be here if she knew he had broken Ruby's heart?

"Stop beating yourself up, Michael. How could you have known dad was having affairs with so many women and that one of them was crazy enough to get back at him by dating you?" Melanie said, pleading with him.

"I lost a chance at real love and happiness," Michael said as he looked over to the table where Ruby and the rest were sitting.

Ruby was smiling at something David was saying. He remembered when she used to smile at him. Now she looked at him with so much hatred. Ruby had made him feel like he was worth loving. She made him feel like he was worth fighting for. Then he'd gone and broken her heart like he knew he would. He didn't deserve her. The best thing he could do for her was let her go. Let her find the love and happiness she deserved to be with someone like Axl.

"Oh, Michael. I understand now, but it's not too late. She's just engaged. She's not married yet," Melanie said as she followed his gaze and knew he was referring to Ruby.

"I don't want to talk about this anymore," Michael said as he stood up and walked away.

"Michael, wait. I'll hang out with you," Cade said as he walked after Michael.

Cade had stood back, watching as Melanie and Michael talked, ready to jump in, in case he was needed.

"I don't need a babysitter," Michael said through gritted teeth as he walked away from Cade.

"Ok, I just wanted to hang out," Cade called out after him.

"Don't take it personally. He's been moody with all of us," Melanie said as she squeezed Cade's hand.

"Michael needs to be careful. He's still on pain medication from his accident. He's been drinking a lot," Cade said, worried.

"Believe me; I'm worried about him, too. But there's no getting through to him right now," Melanie said as they walked back to their table and noticed that Mary Elle had been watching them and had a worried look on her face.

CHAPTER 4

Mary Elle and Wyatt were sitting outside the testing center waiting for Lorraine to finish her GED exam. Wyatt was pacing back and forth, and Mary Elle had anxiously peeled off all her nail polish. They were both a ball of nerves. They knew how much this test meant to Lorraine and for the future; she was trying to create for herself.

The door to the testing center opened, and Lorraine slowly walked over to them. Her face was red, and Mary Elle could tell she'd been crying. Her stomach dropped, and she couldn't think of anything to say.

"Did you pass? Are you ready to sign up for college?" Wyatt asked as soon as Lorraine reached them.

Lorraine broke down and began to cry again. Wyatt looked over at Mary Elle with a confused look on his face.

"I failed again, just like I fail at everything. I can never do anything right!" Lorraine said in between sobs.

"Wyatt, could you wait for us in the car, please?" Mary Elle asked as she dug around her purse for the keys.

She tossed them at Wyatt, and he left without saying a word. He didn't need to say anything. Mary Elle could tell how he was feeling by the looking on his face.

"Look at me," Mary Elle said to Lorraine once Wyatt was out of earshot.

Lorraine slowly raised her gaze and met Mary Elle's.

"You haven't failed. The moment you decide to give up, you fail. You fail the moment you show that boy that after one bump in the road, you stop trying. You only ever fail when you stop trying. Are you going to stop now? You didn't get this far to only get this far. Now you know what to expect. You know what areas you need to work on, so let's go. Get yourself together," Mary Elle said sternly, yet with love, just like a mother.

She was shaking by the time she was done with her pep talk. It had been a while since she had gotten worked up that way, but she refused to see anyone give up, especially so close to the finish line.

"You really think I can do this?"

"I don't think you can do this, Lorraine. I know you can, and you will accomplish so much more than you can even imagine right now."

Lorraine wiped the tears that had dried on her face. "Thank you. No one's ever talked to me that way. No one's ever believed in me before. My family thought I was just a dumb girl. Especially after I got pregnant, no one thought I'd be able to raise Wyatt or give him a wonderful future, and they were right."

Mary Elle felt her chest tighten. She didn't know what it was like to grow up without support. To grow up thinking you were a failure and that no matter what you did, it would never be enough. She wanted Lorraine to see herself the way she did. She'd survived so much, and she was still standing and trying. Lorraine was stronger than anyone she'd ever known.

"You have a long list of people that believe in you now, Lorraine. We will support you every step of the way because you are a part of our family now. You're not doing this alone anymore."

"Thank you," Lorraine whispered as she hugged Mary Elle.

Once Lorraine was ready to talk, she and Mary Elle reviewed her test results. She had only missed a few points in math. Lorraine had done well on all other subjects.

"Your scores aren't bad," Mary Elle said as she looked at the results.

"Yeah, I didn't really look at them until now. I just saw that I failed and broke down."

"We'll show Brandon your test results, so he knows what areas to focus on for your tutoring. Next time you'll ace this. This was just a practice run."

"I feel ashamed, but I know Brandon will understand. I was so nervous about taking the test. Next time I have to take my time," Lorraine said as she got into Mary Elle's car, where Wyatt had patiently waited for them.

"Mom, I'm so proud of you. I know you failed, but the important thing is that you aren't giving up. That means so much." Wyatt said as he gave Lorraine's shoulder a tender squeeze.

"Thank you, Wyatt," Lorraine said as she placed her hand over his and smiled. Things in Lorraine's life were falling back into place. Her life had been chaotic, but recently with Mary Elle's and Thomas' help, everything was shifting to a positive new future for her and Wyatt.

"It's a blessing to see you both bonding and, in a way, growing up together," Mary Elle said as she looked over at them as she got in the driver's seat of her car.

"Thanks to you and Thomas; without you guys, we wouldn't have been able to be here," Wyatt said as he smiled at Mary Elle.

* * *

"MICHAEL," Tiffany said as she softly knocked on his bedroom door.

"Come in," Michael said as he sat up on his bed. The curtains were drawn, and his room was dark.

It was easy to tell he was going through a dark period in his life. Michael had been withdrawn and drinking most days and nights. He would sometimes stay up super late playing video games and sleep for hours afterward. He wasn't usually like this; Michael had always enjoyed working and growing his business and moving forward in his career. He was very similar to Bill. Now, Michael was always home, depressed, and with no motivation.

"I wanted to know if you would like to join us in the lake house. We'll have BBQ, go fishing and just have fun," Tiffany asked, hoping he would join them.

She felt guilty in a way. She had been rude and distant from him since she went through Ruby's phone. There was so much unfinished business, and she knew she had handled it all wrong. She loved her brother, but she knew he wasn't ready for a relationship with Ruby yet. He needed to heal himself first. Ruby deserved the best version of her brother.

"I'm not interested. I need to catch up on some things," Michael replied without even looking at her. He did not feel like being around others. For now, he had to deal with himself first.

"Ok, well, if you change your mind, you know where you can find us. For what it's worth, I'm sorry for being distant. I know I was wrong, and I should have been more understanding and kind. It's difficult discovering the truth about someone you thought you loved and were supposed to marry. I also know that the person you truly love is out there, and she loves you back, but the timing was all wrong," Tiffany said, blurting all her thoughts out as if the floodgates had given way, and she could express all of this at once.

"Tiffany, I'll think about going," Michael said.

Tiffany felt sadness inside of her heart for him. She knew he was devastated, and most, including Ruby, had turned their backs on him. As she left Mary Elle's house, she thought about ways to help Michael. His drinking was not under control anymore. Mary Elle and Thomas had already spoken to him about it, and he had stopped drinking every day, but it was still something he used when he felt all the darkness move back into his mind and heart. Mary Elle had been praying and asking God to heal Michael's heart. He had lost his fiancé, and he felt anger and even hatred towards Samantha. He never expected to be used as revenge for his father, Bill. His relationship with Bill had been strong before. They would often bond over work commitments, and both enjoyed playing golf and meeting with father-son businesses, as they, too, had their own father-son company. Michael knew Bill had affairs, but he never knew about his affair with Samantha.

Tiffany was still confused about the messages she'd seen on Ruby's phone. Michael and Ruby had known each other since childhood. Ruby was one of his sisters' best friends. She was always around for birthdays, holidays, school, summer, and family vacations. Ruby had always been shy, quiet, fun, and extremely smart. Her parents were honest and hard-working. Ruby was raised in a pleasant home as a single child; her brother Simon had passed away from a congenital heart defect. Her parents decided not to have any more children after that. Throughout the years, Michael had seen Ruby grow into a beautiful young lady. He saw her go through her ugly duckling phase with braces and glasses, then through her teen years with bad acne, and he felt nothing more than friendship towards her. Michael was a few years older than Ruby and started dating girls in his teen years. Michael didn't go through awkward years. He was always handsome and charming. Girls always liked him and were drawn to him. In high school, Michael played basketball and was popular. During college, he continued to play basketball and dated all the gorgeous cheerleaders on campus. He was a ladies' man, and he had never gotten his heart broken until now. So, when did things change between them?

* * *

"Come on, ladies! Keep up!" Mrs. Adelman called from the front of the group.

"Are you trying to kill us?" one lady called out.

Melanie tried her best to stifle a giggle. She joined Mrs. Adelman's walking club to lose some weight she had gained during her pregnancy with Ryder. Now that she was pregnant again, she knew she had to be better about exercising and giving in to cravings. She refused to keep torturing herself at the gym with Tiffany.

Ruby was walking next to Melanie, and her cheeks were flushed. "I thought you said she was in her 70s!" she said as she wiped the sweat off her forehead.

"She is, but still much more energetic and in shape than us," Melanie said as she stopped to drink some water.

Ruby stopped next to her and watched as the rest of the ladies passed them. They were a sight to be seen with their florescent colored sun protection athleisure outfits. "That's going to be us one day," Ruby said as she watched a group of three older women zoom past them with their handy walking sticks.

"I hope we'll still be in each other's lives then," Melanie said, thinking out loud.

Ruby turned to her with a shocked and hurt expression on her face. "What do you mean? Of course, we will be."

"What's going on between you and Michael, Ruby?"

Ruby turned away from her and looked out at the vastness of the mountains. "Nothing's going on between us."

Melanie rolled her eyes. She was tired of playing dumb and pretending she didn't know about the texts between Tiffany and Michael. Still, she couldn't tell Ruby that Tiffany had broken her trust. "Ruby, it's obvious to all of us that there's more going on."

"Mel, it's complicated. I don't want to talk about it right now, not here," Ruby said as she gulped water from her insulated water bottle.

"It's not that I mean to invade your privacy, but it's clearly affecting my brother, and it needs to be addressed. Ruby, you're one of my best friends, and I also love you. I don't want Michael to hurt you or for you to hurt him. I know things might be complicated, but talking things through always helps find a solution," Melanie said as she looked at Ruby.

"Come on, ladies, don't stay too far behind," Mrs. Adelman shouted as she looked back at them.

"Mel, I love you and your family. It's never been my intention to hurt any of you, especially not Michael. You know I've had a crush on him since we were kids. I know how he is, but I still loved him and have always prayed that God would bring him peace and help him find a good woman to settle down with. That's always been my prayer. I just wish he could see himself for who he truly is," Ruby said as she started towards Mrs. Adelman to catch up with her.

"I don't mean to butt in, Ruby. I just love you both and hate seeing you like this," Melanie said as she, too, started toward Mrs. Adelman and the rest of the group.

CHAPTER 5

"What's going on?" David asked Tiffany as he poured food for the cows and pigs.

"Nothing," Tiffany said, flashing him a smile and continued pouring out some fresh hay.

"You've been quiet all day. What's going on?" David asked her again.

Tiffany sighed as she petted MooMoo, her favorite cow.

"I just feel bad that I've been so harsh on Michael. He's my brother, and I should be there for him. I shouldn't have judged him or his choices. I should've been more understanding."

"I agree, but you shouldn't get down about it. It's not like you to give up. Talk things out and work on your relationship."

"You agree?" Tiffany said with a small laugh. She was hoping that he would tell her she was wrong, that she hadn't been too hard on Michael.

"Tiff, you hold everyone to very high standards..." David began and held his hands up in defense as Tiffany watched him with a raised brow. "Let me finish," he said with a laugh.

"Go on..." Tiffany said, tilting her head to the side.

"You hold everyone to very high standards, which isn't a bad thing, but you need to realize that no one is perfect. You do it to yourself as well, and you beat yourself up when you don't meet your own expectations. All I'm saying is that you should show your brother a little grace. He's going through a lot."

"Yes, I can see what you're trying to say. It's just hard, I guess. I know Michael could be so much better, but he stops himself. He sells himself short. He's so stubborn and keeps to himself that no one knows what's happening. Sometimes I feel like there is a small rain cloud hanging over his head that he purposely puts there to not let himself enjoy life."

"Maybe he doesn't think he deserves a good life."

"Why would he think that?" Tiffany asked, jumping up. She'd often thought that about Michael, but she could never understand why he would sabotage himself. Why did he think he didn't deserve to be happy?

"I don't know, but you'll never know if you don't talk things out with him."

"You're right. Thanks for always listening," Tiffany said as she placed a kiss on his cheek.

"Are you ready for our picnic?" David asked her.

"Yes, I'm starving!" Tiffany said as she shook the hay off of herself.

David went to his car to grab the food he'd prepared for them and a blanket to sit on. They set themselves up near the lake at the back of the farm.

"Mr. Gallows is thinking of selling his farm and land," David said.

Tiffany looked over to the farm next door. It was much bigger than David's.

"I hope someone local buys it. I'd hate for some big-shot developer to take it."

"I was thinking of buying it from him. He said I could pay him directly with no interest instead of going through a bank."

"What would you do with all that land?"

"I don't know yet, but it would be a shame not to buy it."

"I'm sure that whatever you decide to do will be great," Tiffany said, giving him a light kiss on the lips.

It was days like these that made Willow Heights feel like heaven on earth. Everything was as it should be, and the best was yet to come. She would figure out a way to talk to Michael and help him. He needed to realize that he deserved to have a happy life, too. Life was too short to hold yourself back from love and happiness.

* * *

"MICHAEL, I've made your favorite peach cobbler," Mary Elle said as she popped her head out the door to where Michael was sitting in the backyard.

"I'll be right in," Michael called out to Mary Elle.

He had been outside, trying to gather his thoughts. It had been about a month since he was in Willow Heights. He was still trying to figure out what to do about work. He lost his job after the car accident, and he didn't know where to go from there. Michael was still trying to figure out Samantha's purpose in using him to get back at Bill. He felt betrayed, disgusted, used, and so many other things he couldn't even wrap his head around, but most of all, he felt anger and hatred.

He didn't like feeling this way, especially towards his father. Michael knew deep down Bill wasn't to blame for what Samantha did and how she used him. He was just angry that Bill had this affair hidden from him and that this had happened. Michael was now realizing the pain and suffering his mother had felt once she had learned about the affair and continued to feel the new revelation of the additional ones she wasn't aware of.

"Here you go; I hope you enjoy it," Mary Elle said as she placed a plate on the dining table for Michael with some iced tea.

"Thank you, mom. I've been distant and avoiding people not to speak about my feelings because I'm not ready to do so yet, but I wanted to thank you for all you've done for me. After what I've been through, I now understand the pain and heartbreak you've had to experience, and I don't know how you did it. I now understand all the wrongs I've done with the women I led on," Michael said as he approached Mary Elle and gave her a bear hug. Michael was tall with a muscular build and towered over Mary Elle. She loved his big bear hugs.

Michael hadn't dated a lot, contrary to what people might believe. Women gravitated to him, and he sometimes flirted because, at the end of the day, he was a man and enjoyed the attention, but he'd only had a couple of relationships.

"Honey, I know you are learning and dealing with many things. You're still trying to figure things out. You are my son, and I love you with all of my heart and only wish the best for you. In time, you'll see that going through this has strengthened you and has given you compassion for others, and you'll also be wiser with women you choose to date," Mary Elle said as she sat down in front of Michael to eat some peach cobbler pie with him.

"I understand that everyone's worried about me. I feel like such a fool for letting this happen with Samantha. When I began my relationship with Samantha, I went into it for all the wrong reasons. I made mistakes with Ruby as well, and I don't think I'll ever be able to fix things with her. There was a time when we were getting close, and I really thought things between us would develop, but then I messed everything up. Everything Ruby and I had been working on came to a standstill, and now she's moved on. I realized she was the one I needed all this time, but I messed up. She hates me because I broke her heart, and I hate myself for it. I know I shouldn't be upset at dad, but I'm upset that he lied about his affairs. He repeatedly broke your heart and trust without even feeling an ounce of remorse. I hated keeping his secrets from you but felt that you not knowing was better than finding out what a scum he was. I had admired dad for so long and for so many reasons but finding out who he really took a toll on me as well," Michael said as he looked at the delicious peach cobbler, realizing all that he had kept inside and was just now ready to open up to his mother.

"Michael, I never knew you felt this way…." Mary Elle said as she moved closer to him.

"It's been difficult. I wanted to protect you, and I wanted to believe he would change or come clean. Then you learned about his affair when he didn't even show up for his birthday party. That was the turning point for me. He chose others over us. It was no longer just about you and him. He also shut me down, which broke my heart," Michael said, as some tears filled his eyes.

Michael had always held his father, Bill, in high esteem, and although their relationship had been rocky during Michael's teenage years. It was then that Michael witnessed Bill's affairs firsthand. He didn't want to break Mary Elle's heart. Michael had demanded that Bill stop seeing women on the side, but Bill told him he was in no position to demand anything from him. The affairs continued, and it was as if Bill paraded them and put them on display for Michael to see.

"It was never your job to keep secrets or to protect me,"

Mary Elle said as she felt the anguish Michael was expressing.

"I know, mom, but I felt powerless and disgusted. But then again, I couldn't judge him. I was just like him, in a way. I've always been insensitive towards women and have respected none of them except you, my sisters, and Ruby. That's why with Ruby, I was taking things slow. I didn't want to mess it up. I didn't want to hurt her or rush into things as I have in the past," Michael said, looking at Mary Elle in the eyes with a sad smile on his face. It was clear he loved them and never intended to hurt them, but now it was too late.

"Darling, we just need to fix things. We need to talk things out and move forward," Mary Elle said.

"I'm not ready. I don't know that I deserve any chances to fix things, especially with Ruby. She's moved on and is engaged. I don't want to cause more problems for her. She was always the one I would talk to and open up to when I had all these things going on. She has always kept quiet and not said anything to you or my sisters," Michael said, letting whatever he felt had been weighing him down out in the open.

"That must have been a burden on her as well. I know it must've been difficult for her, too. Your father should've never placed you in that position," Mary Elle said with fire in her eyes.

CHAPTER 6

"Thomas, I am stepping out for a few hours," Mary Elle said, poking her head inside his office. She hadn't been able to think straight since her last conversation with Michael. She had a fire burning inside of her and had been arguing with Bill in her head all day. There were so many things she needed to say to him, and she would not stop until he understood the damage he had caused their son.

When she noticed Thomas was sitting at his desk with his hands holding his head up, she came inside. She felt the anger inside her subside and replaced with a concern for Thomas' well-being.

"What's wrong she asked?"

"Dean just gave me his two weeks' notice," Thomas said, sounding defeated.

"Dean? Why?" Mary Elle asked, confused.

Dean was like a son to Thomas. He'd given him a chance to work for him when no one else had.

"He wants to focus on his food truck."

"I see," Mary Elle said.

She knew how excited Dean had been when he had

finally raised enough money to buy his food truck. He had been working endlessly to get it up and running. It was hard to upset him for wanting to follow his dream.

"First Patty, now Dean..." Thomas said softly.

"We'll figure this out. We always do. I can always get put my trusty apron on and do my part," Mary Elle said, flashing him a smile.

"Of course, you would," Thomas said with a sad smile. He pulled Mary Elle onto his lap and hugged her close.

"It's not like you to let life get you down, Thomas. Let's put a job posting up. Let's get to work," Mary Elle said, raising his chin.

"Maybe this was a ploy to get you in my arms..." Thomas said with a wink.

Mary Elle giggled and said, "You silly man. What would I do without you?"

"What would I do without you? Where were you going anyway?" Thomas asked.

"It can wait," Mary Elle said, suddenly not interested in having anything to do with Bill.

This is where she belonged. Everyone that she loved and held dear was here in Willow Heights. She was done with letting Bill steal her joy and peace. Nothing could be said or done about the things that happened in the past. What mattered was now, and right now, the man she loved needed her.

* * *

"How is your coffee, dad?" DeeAnn asked as she saw Greggory set the coffee back down on the table with a shaky hand.

He had been silent all morning, and she constantly found

him spacing out, lost in thought. DeeAnn was worried that might be feeling down.

"Everything is wonderful," he said and tried to give her a reassuring smile.

"Once we're done with breakfast, we can go to Paul's produce farm. He said he could use your help today."

Greggory's face lit up just a little at the mention of the produce farm. They'd been going every other day for the last few weeks. Paul gave Greggory minor tasks he could complete, like picking some of the produce, and when it had been very hot outside one day, he let Greggory look over the farm's finances.

Being productive and working brought some life back to Greggory. She couldn't imagine what it must be like for him to depend so much on others now as he did. He had always been a very independent, hard-working man, and he'd always taken great pride in that.

Now that he was needing help to walk, go to the bathroom, and all the other things he'd been able to do without a second thought, he was having a hard time accepting help and adjusting. He'd had a fit when Sheila told him he needed to wear a diaper. He had an even bigger fit when it was time to change it.

What many didn't understand was how this affected Sheila as well. It wasn't easy for her to see their father struggle. He'd always been her hero; he'd always seemed unbreakable to her. In his prime, Greggory had been a force to reckon with. He was unstoppable and had a zest for life that made everyone around him want to be better.

Once they finished breakfast, DeeAnn got her father into her compact sedan. It was a bit of a struggle, but a few minutes later, they were on the road. She was considering getting a small SUV because that might be easier to get him in and out of. DeeAnn looked over at Greggory and smiled.

She loved the way he lit up when he went to the farm. More than anything, she loved the relationship her father and Paul shared. Paul was waiting outside for them as they drove up. He had a smile on his face, and DeeAnn couldn't help but notice how much more fit he seemed. Working at the produce farm was doing wonders for his physique.

"If it isn't my favorite farm hand and his beautiful daughter," Paul said as he helped Greggory out of the car. He made it seem so effortless. DeeAnn stood back and observed, hoping to learn a thing or two.

"A lot of work today?" Greggory asked as he pushed his walker towards the fields.

Sheila and DeeAnn felt more comfortable pushing Greggory in his wheelchair, but Paul gave him more freedom by letting him walk with his walker.

"Work here is never done. When I think I'm finally all caught up, about ten more things pop up," Paul said with a tired laugh.

"Good thing we're here then," DeeAnn heard Greggory say to Paul.

DeeAnn watched as the men went on their way to get to work. She went the other way toward the small office. She had tried working out in the field with them a few times, but it just wasn't for her. DeeAnn preferred working indoors with air conditioning, which was much nicer for her curly hair than the heat and humidity.

"Good morning, Rachel," DeeAnn said to the young assistant that managed the office.

When Paul purchased the produce farm, he had kept all the staff on board. DeeAnn thought he could do without some of the staff and save some of the money from their salary, but he didn't think it was fair to displace them when they were doing a great job at helping him run the farm.

"Hi DeeAnn, I didn't know you were coming today."

"My dad likes to help, and I have him today," DeeAnn said with a shrug.

"I'll make sure to take him some water in a bit," Rachel said as she resumed her administrative duties.

DeeAnn didn't know why she felt insecure about Rachel working with Paul. Maybe it was because she was younger than her, and she got to spend so much more time with him than she did. She hadn't seen any interaction between them to validate her insecurities; she had to get it together. Rachel was a sweet girl, and she was just doing her job.

DeeAnn organized the office and did some light cleaning before heading to Paul's office to work on bills. She might not be much help on the field, but she enjoyed taking some paperwork load off of him. One of her favorite things was to go through the bills and see where she could save him money. When Paul purchased the farm, the previous owner was behind on bills. DeeAnn had contacted the different vendors and gotten some of the late fees taken off. She'd gotten the farm up to date with all its expenses in no time. It had been the least she could do while Paul dealt with so much more that came with running the produce farm.

"It's hot out there," Paul said as he pushed Greggory in on his wheelchair.

"Is he okay?" DeeAnn asked as she walked over to her father.

He was drenched in sweat and looked pale.

"I'm fine," Greggory said, swatting her hand away from his face.

Rachel appeared with a glass of water, and DeeAnn gave her a grateful smile.

"Drink up," Rachel said as she handed Greggory the glass. He tried to take it from her, but before they knew it, the glass fell to the ground and shattered at their feet.

"Sorry," Greggory said, with tears in his eyes.

"It's okay, don't worry," DeeAnn said as she and Rachel sprang into action, cleaning the mess up.

"Happens to all of us," Paul said as he reappeared with some water for Greggory in a plastic cup.

This time Greggory took it carefully with his shaky hands and took a slow, long drink.

"Are you ready to head home?" DeeAnn asked him.

"I thought the three of us could have lunch at Willow Acres," Paul said.

"Lunch sounds like a good idea," Greggory said.

"I can't argue with that," DeeAnn said as she gave Paul a side hug and placed a kiss on his cheek.

CHAPTER 7

Rita and Sienna were packing up online orders that had come in overnight when Wyatt walked into the store.

"Hi there, Wyatt. What brings you here?" Rita asked as he approached the counter.

"Do you still have the resin necklace with the flowers?" Wyatt asked as he looked around the shop.

"I think he means the birth month flower bouquet necklaces," Sienna said as she walked over to the display.

Wyatt followed her, and his face lit up when he saw them.

"I would like two, one for Rosie and one for my mom."

"Which months?" Rita asked as she pulled out a small box and ribbon to package them up with.

"Actually... I think I'll only take one," Wyatt said quietly.

"Oh? Why?" Rita asked, concerned at the shift in his mood.

"I can only afford one right now, but I'll come back when I have enough for the other one," Wyatt said.

"Nonsense! You get a friend and family discount," Rita told him.

"No, I want to support you."

"And you are. When people see Lorraine and Rosie out and about, they'll ask them about their necklaces and refer them to the shop."

"Are you sure?" Wyatt asked.

"I've never been surer."

"Thanks!" Wyatt said excitedly again.

He picked out the two necklaces that he wanted, and Rita packaged them up for him. She even threw up gift bags that she usually charged extra for, but she didn't tell him. Wyatt came around the counter and gave Rita a big hug, and thanked her. He waved bye to Sienna and was on his way.

"What a sweet boy," Sienna said.

"He is so great. Lorraine did a fantastic job with him."

"I've yet to meet her, but the girls tell me she's trying to get her life together."

"Yeah, she is. Mary Elle and Thomas are helping her get her high school diploma. Then I heard she wants to go into nursing like you."

"That's fantastic. Nursing is such a rewarding career. I can give her my textbooks. I think they're still using the same ones."

"That would be great. Thank you, sweetheart."

"Of course. Oh, look at the time. I have to get back to work. I can come by after work to help you pack up any orders that come in throughout the day."

"I'd appreciate that. Thank you. Tell the Banks I say hello!"

Rita wondered what her life would've been like if she'd been placed in Lorraine's shoes. What if her parents had let her keep Sienna? Where would she be now? Would she and Robert still be together? How different would their lives have been? Lorraine was much stronger than she knew. She raised a wonderful boy and was getting her life back on track now.

When many would've given up, she stood tall. Rita would always hold the utmost respect for single mothers everywhere, especially those that raised kids while they were still kids themselves, like Lorraine.

* * *

"So..." Tiffany said as she spread some gel nail polish over Ruby's nails. It was her day off, and they spent it in Willow Acres because that's where all their favorite people were.

Tiffany had brought her gel nail polish kit with her, and they were sitting by the lake towards the back of the restaurant, where there was an outlet for her UV lamp.

"So..." Ruby said.

Tiffany let out a sigh. Ruby was her very best friend, and she was worried that she would ruin their friendship because she'd been acting so awkwardly for the last few weeks. She couldn't help it. She felt guilty for breaking her trust, but she felt even worse, thinking that there might have been something going on between Ruby and Michael before that she'd never known about. Tiffany thought they told each other everything.

"Brandon will visit soon. I think he's flying in today," Tiffany said, trying to come up with something to talk about.

Brandon was one of Michael's college friends and roommate. He had also moved to California after college and was one of Michael's best friends.

"That's good for Michael," Ruby said nonchalantly.

Tiffany let out an exasperated sigh. What would it take to get Ruby talking? Why didn't she trust her?

"What's wrong? Do you not like Brandon?" Ruby asked, confused by Tiffany's reaction.

"No, Brandon is great. He's probably the only one of

Michael's friends that I actually like," Tiffany said as she moved on to Ruby's other hand.

"So, what's bothering you? You've been acting strange. Are things okay between you and David?"

"Things between us have never been better. What about you and Axl? Where is he?" Tiffany asked. She hoped that this would get Ruby talking.

"He's on a work trip. Things are good. He's a good man."

"Do you love him?" Tiffany asked before she could stop herself.

"I'm engaged to him," Ruby said, sitting up and adjusting her top.

"Yes, but are you in love with him?" Tiffany asked again, gentler this time.

"He's a great man, Tiffany. He loves me," Ruby said as a tear streamed down her face.

"Ruby..." Tiffany began before Wyatt interrupted them.

"Would you like a refill?" He asked, pointing at their empty sweet tea glasses.

"No, we were getting ready to leave," Ruby said, flashing him a smile.

"Okay, see you around," he said before disappearing again.

"Are you ready to go?" Ruby asked as she inspected her manicured nails.

"We need to talk about this," Tiffany said as she put her nail polishes away.

"There's nothing to talk about," Ruby said.

"Hello, ladies," Jasper said, sitting at the table next to them. He took his hat off and placed it on the table. He ran his hands over his short, wavy hair.

"How's it going?" Tiffany asked him.

She had seen little of him now that Britney didn't come

around as often. Jasper always kept to himself, but Britney had gotten him out of his shell.

"Everything is good. Needed a break because it's too hot out there," he said.

"How's Britney? I haven't talked to her lately. Where in the world is she now?" Ruby asked with a small laugh.

Britney was Melanie's friend from New York. She had a travel blog and wrote travel columns for the magazine Melanie had worked at during her time in New York. While helping Melanie plan her wedding, Britney and Jasper had hit it off.

"I wouldn't know..." Jasper said, taking a sip of water.

"She'll come around, Jasp," Tiffany said.

She felt for Jasper. He was such an amazing guy, and he was such a great match for Britney, but she still had some healing and growing to do.

"All we can do is pray for her. Anyway, my break is over. I'll see you, ladies, around," he said with a sad smile.

"See you," Ruby said as she shifted in her seat and looked around as if trying to escape Tiffany.

"Hold on, Ruby," Tiffany said as she noticed Ruby's reaction.

"Tif, I just don't want to talk about it here. Can we talk about it somewhere else?"

"Sure, I know just the spot," Tiffany said as she gathered her things and placed them in her small tote.

The girls walked over behind the restaurant, near one of the gardens. They chose a nice quiet spot shaded by a beautiful willow tree and sat down under its shade.

"Ruby, I'm not trying to judge or pressure you. I'm your best friend, and all I ever want for you is to be happy. Are you in love with Axl?" Tiffany asked her without hesitation.

"No. I don't love him," Ruby said as her eyes filled with tears and her smile turned into a frown.

"Then why are you engaged to him?"

"He's been there for me. He's a good man, and I just don't want to be alone anymore."

"That's no reason to be with someone who doesn't make you happy. I can see it. You sometimes even look bothered when he calls or sends you text messages. That's not what a happy couple should look like. You're still young, beautiful, and you shouldn't settle just because you don't want to be alone," Tiffany said as she hugged her best friend and wiped some tears off her face.

"The man I'm in love with has broken my heart into a million pieces. He led me on, and I fell for him. I had always loved him, but he only ever saw me as a friend, then suddenly things changed, and we were dating, and then bam! It was all gone again. I feel ashamed. I gave my heart to him, and all he did was break it. Under the guise that he was doing what he thought was best for me. If he was doing what was best for me, why did he dump me and immediately get engaged to someone else? Then I met Axl, and our relationship has been a whirlwind, but I felt like it was real, and he's a safe choice."

It was at this moment that Tiffany started realizing Ruby and Michael had dated, and he had broken her heart. She became furious to think that he would do such a thing to Ruby, her best friend, and although he's her brother, she was angered to think he would cause Ruby such pain.

"Ruby, are you talking about Michael?"

"Yes, I've always been in love with him, but I've always known that he is not the type of man to settle down with someone like me. I'm not the gorgeous cheerleader or the sexy flight attendant. I'm just plain Jane."

"Ruby, don't say that! You are beautiful, kind, smart, genuine, total wife material, not just a one-night stand or a summer fling. Michael always chooses the wrong type of girl. Look where it landed him. I love you, and I love him, but maybe you're better off without him," Tiffany said as lovingly as she could.

"He's a very special guy. It's just that few people see that side of him. He's also tender and caring. When we dated briefly, he always made me feel important and safe. I never doubted him, but after the camping trip with everyone, things changed. I don't know what Samantha said or did to him, but being an older woman, I'm sure she knew what she was doing to manipulate him and get the revenge she desired from your father."

"I know Michael's not a bad person. I know he must have cared for you. Maybe there's a way to work things out?" Tiffany asked.

"I don't know, Tiffany. Maybe I'm stubborn, but when all this went down with him and your father and Samantha, I felt like it was what he deserved. But deep down, I felt sadness for him. He reached out to me, and I just ignored him. Right after he broke up with me, he flew to Atlanta and apologized. He said he had messed up and that he loved me. Michael begged me to take him back, but I was too proud. Then, suddenly, he got engaged to Samantha. Not telling you and Melanie was the hardest thing I ever had to do. I had to smile and pretend everything was okay during Christmas and Melanie's wedding, but inside, it hurt so much."

"I'm so sorry, Ruby…." Tiffany said as she got even angrier at Michael.

"When I met Axl, I just wanted to forget about Michael, so I jumped right in. I know that was a horrible thing to do, but I thought I was protecting myself from getting hurt again, and maybe all that Michael needed was a friend. I wasn't there for him. Then he spiraled downward, hit rock bottom, and had that car accident, and we almost lost him. I felt like I was to blame for that, in a way. I wanted to be there for him, but again, my stubbornness has kept me from being a true friend to him. Axl visiting and everything else just makes me feel worse. I know I shouldn't be with Axl because I don't love him the way he wants me to, but I'm being selfish and want to be wanted and loved."

"Michael is a complicated person, Ruby. I've always felt like he sabotages himself from being truly happy. I don't know what made him this way. What I know is that you don't need to rush towards anything with anyone, Ruby," Tiffany said. She knew she probably shouldn't be saying that, but she still wasn't convinced that Michael was the right person for Ruby.

"I'm realizing that now. I don't know what I was thinking," Ruby said in a shameful tone.

CHAPTER 8

"Splish splash!" Melanie said as she played with Ryder at the edge of the lake.

Ryder let out a giggle, and Ruby couldn't help but smile. He was the cutest little boy she'd ever seen. Ryder grabbed his rubber dinosaur and placed it on Ruby's lap. Thomas had gotten him the dinosaur for his first birthday, which was his favorite. He took it with him everywhere he went.

"Is it mine now?" Ruby asked, holding the Dino close to her chest.

Ryder looked like he was going to cry when he heard her say that.

"You can share, Ry," Melanie said and kissed his head.

Ryder smiled and continued to splash the water. They were celebrating that Michael's friend Brandon was visiting. They'd brought out the kayaks and floats for a day on the lake. David and Cade were setting up a grill. Thomas would come by with his boat later and jet skis. Everyone was having a good time, and, for the first time in a long time, Ruby didn't feel conflicted. She felt relieved that she had finally come clean to Tiffany yesterday about her feelings for Michael.

"Hey, where'd you go?" Melanie asked, bringing her back to the present moment.

"I was just thinking..."

"About?" Melanie asked with a raised brow.

"This is nice. I wish every day were like today."

"Me too. It feels like the old times but better because now we have some recent additions," Melanie said as she gazed over at Cade.

It really felt like the good old days when they were kids and could spend all day together in the summer.

"Even Michael looks happy," Melanie said, cutting into Ruby's thoughts again.

Ruby had been trying her hardest not to look at where Michael was, but now that Melanie brought him up, she stole a glance over at him. He was sitting with Brandon, David, and Cade near the grill. He seemed like he didn't have a care in the world. Ruby smiled as he laughed at something Brandon said. She loved seeing him happy. He deserved it so much. Michael must have felt her looking at him because he turned, and their eyes locked. She felt a blush creep up her cheeks, but she couldn't look away. He smiled at her, and she smiled back, but then something hit her on the side of the head.

"Ryder, no!" Melanie said.

"It's okay," Ruby said, picking Ryder up and handing his dinosaur back to him.

"Would you ladies like some water?" Brandon asked as he approached them, with Michael closed behind.

"Thanks," Melanie said, taking the bottled waters from him.

"So, what do you think of Willow Heights?" Ruby asked him.

"It couldn't be more different from California, but I can see the appeal."

"Maybe you can convince my brother to move here," Melanie said.

Michael chuckled, but didn't say a word.

"He said that he was looking for a change..." Brandon said with a small laugh.

"Anyone hungry?" Cade asked, interrupting the group.

"When aren't I hungry?" Melanie asked, looking down at her baby bump.

"Hot dogs or burgers?" Cade asked them.

Melanie and Ruby stood and followed the guys to the tables.

The guys had been in charge of the food, and it smelled really delicious. Aside from the burgers and hot dogs, they had different sodas, chips, potato salad, macaroni salad, and even a fruit salad they probably bought pre-made.

"Are you having fun?" Michael asked.

"Yeah, are you?" Ruby asked, looking around. Just then, a breeze blew, and Ruby caught the scent of Michael's cologne. That scent was so familiar to her. He'd worn the same one since high school.

She didn't like the way she felt when she was around him. Ruby thought that after all this time, things would be different. She was engaged, yet she was still acting like that little girl that always had a crush on her best friend's older brother.

"Yeah, it's good to be around family. It's good to be around you."

Ruby felt a blush coming on, and she looked down at her feet. She didn't know what to say.

Michael cleared his throat and said, "Being around you reminds me of the good old days. Back when we were all happy, and things were simple."

Ruby met his gaze and wanted nothing more than to hug him, but she knew better.

"Things will get better for you," she said instead and quickly left to where Tiffany and Melanie were.

* * *

After a wonderful day at the lake, the group went to Tiffany and DeeAnn's place to unwind. They weren't ready for the day to end. DeeAnn was out with Paul for date night. Mary Elle and Thomas had taken Ryder with them to their place.

"Should we play truth or dare for old times' sake?" Tiffany asked with an evil laugh.

Michael groaned and playfully threw a cushion at Tiffany's head.

"Hey, watch it!" she said.

"It might be fun..." Melanie said with a playful smile.

"What if we watch a movie instead?" David asked, noticing none of the guys were into the idea of playing truth or dare.

"Or... we could play a board game," Melanie said.

The girls were never into the same movies that the guys liked. Most of the time, they took longer picking out a movie than actually watching it.

"I've got an idea," Michael said, sitting up.

Everyone sat up when they saw how his face lit up and heard the excitement in his tone.

"What is it?" Melanie asked suspiciously.

"Let's play hide and seek."

"What?" Melanie asked, unsure that she'd heard right.

"Yes, let's go!" Tiffany said, jumping up and ready to go.

"When did we go back in time and turn ten years old again?" Brandon asked.

"Live a little!" Tiffany and Michael said in unison before looking at each other and breaking out into a smile.

"I don't know if you guys have noticed, but I'm pregnant," Melanie said, pointing at her belly.

"You can make sure that no one cheats," Ruby chimed in.

"Wait, you're taking their side?" Melanie asked in disbelief.

"It sounds like fun..." Ruby said with an impish smile.

"Are you all okay with this?" Melanie asked, turning to Cade, David, and Brandon.

"I was always pretty good at hide and seek," David said with a shrug.

"It's better than watching another boring movie..." Cade said with a smile.

"Fine, fine. You win!" Melanie said, turning to Tiffany and Michael, shaking her head.

"Some things never change," Tiffany said to Michael, loud enough for everyone to hear.

The group played hide and seek, and, true to his claim, David won each time. Tiffany did not know how someone with his stature could hide better than she could. Her competitive streak was coming out. She took advantage of the moment David went to the bathroom to devise a plan with the rest of the group that involved making David lose.

"I just want it to be known that I do not agree with this little plan of yours," Melanie said, shaking her finger at her.

"He has to be cheating. We're just making things fair," Tiffany said, although she felt a little guilty.

Before they could get their plan in motion, there was a knock at the door. Melanie answered the door, and when she returned, she had an unreadable look on her face.

"What's wrong?" Tiffany asks.

"Hi, everyone," Axl says, stepping into the room behind Melanie.

He walks over to Ruby and plants a kiss on her lips in

front of everyone. Tiffany looks at Michael and feels an ache in her chest because of the broken look on his face.

"We were just leaving," Brandon says.

Tiffany looks at him, confused. Does he know about Michael and Tiffany? What does he know?

"Don't go yet! We haven't cut the cake," Tiffany said.

She couldn't let Brandon go without discovering what he knew about her brother and Ruby.

"Whose birthday is it?" Axl asked.

"Mine," Brandon said without so much as a glance over at Axl.

Tiffany felt bad for Axl. He was a nice guy. She'd only met him twice, but he was always nice. It wasn't his fault that her brother was in love with Ruby.

"Brandon... why don't you help Melanie and I bring the cake out?" Tiffany asked, trying not to give anything away.

"How big is the cake?" Michael asked.

Tiffany ignored him and dragged Melanie to the kitchen. Brandon followed them, and as soon as they were out of earshot, Tiffany turned to him and asked him to tell them everything he knew.

"What are you talking about?" he asked, but Tiffany could tell he knew exactly what she was talking about.

"I saw how you acted when Axl came in and kissed Ruby. I also saw the look on my brother's face, and I know you saw it too," she said, not ready to let this go.

Brandon leaned back on the counter and sighed. He looked up at the ceiling and said, "Your brother's been pinning around after Ruby since I met him in college."

Tiffany and Melanie looked at each other in disbelief.

"Are you sure?" Melanie asked.

"Do you know any other Ruby best friends with his little sisters?"

The rest of the night was a blur for Tiffany. Laying in her

bed, she thought about what Brandon had told them. How in the world had she not known that her brother had been in love with her best friend all these years? According to Brandon, Michael never dated in college and only lied about it to his family. Apart from Samantha, he hadn't really dated many other girls. Michael had told him he didn't want to be like Bill. He didn't want to hurt women or use them as his father had. All these years, Tiffany believed her brother to be a player, but it was all a lie. How had she not caught on?

CHAPTER 9

Thomas was hard at work when Mary Elle stepped into his office. He looked up from the mess of papers on his desk and smiled at her.

"What brings you here?" He asked her.

"I was just thinking...it's been a while since we had alone time."

"You've been busy," he said with a shrug.

"Yes, but I feel bad, and I don't want you to feel you're not a priority for me because you are."

Thomas stood and walked over to her. He took her hands and said, "Michael is your son, and he needs you right now. I completely understand that. You shouldn't feel bad."

"Thank you. Still, how do you feel about getting away for the weekend? Just the two of us?"

Mary Elle could sense hesitation in Thomas, and she felt her stomach knotting. She knew it wasn't easy for Thomas to be away from here.

"Where were you thinking?" he asked, to her surprise.

"I was thinking somewhere new, something different...

maybe a beach resort?" Mary Elle said as she twirled her floral flowy sundress.

Mary Elle loved wearing sundresses during the summer. Thomas always complimented her sundresses and loved her fashion sense.

"Alright, sweetheart. We can go wherever you take us, surprise me," Thomas said as he hugged Mary Elle and planted a kiss on her head.

Mary Elle left the office in a great mood. She was sitting outside the testing center with Wyatt, waiting for Lorraine to finish her exam. She had a good feeling about today and was sure that this time Lorraine would pass.

Mary Elle was on her phone looking for all-inclusive beach resorts that wouldn't break their budget when Lorraine came out of the building. Wyatt jumped up and ran towards her, and Mary Elle followed close behind.

"Did you pass?" Wyatt asked, unable to hide his excitement.

Lorraine's eyes welled up, and she nodded excitedly.

Wyatt jumped up and down, hugging her, and Mary Elle joined in too.

"I am so proud of you," Mary Elle said as she hugged Lorraine.

"Thank you, Mary Elle. Thank you for believing in me. I can never repay you and Thomas," Lorraine said with tears in her eyes.

"You don't owe us a thing," Mary Elle said, giving her another hug.

"No one's ever believed in me before. I never thought this would be something I could now. Now I can go to college!" Lorraine said, laughing.

* * *

Ruby and Tiffany met at the Farmer's Market early to select some fresh produce and fruits for the Inn. The Farmer's Market took place on weekends at the Main Square. It had grown exponentially since they had moved to Willow Heights. Axl stayed home working on a report for work. Tiffany was glad to get Ruby to herself. She wanted to know what was happening and if she'd made any decisions.

"How are you feeling, Ruby?" Tiffany asked, knowing Ruby wasn't expecting Axl to visit this weekend.

"Surprised, to say the least. I just don't want to break up with Axl. I don't want to confront him or hurt his feelings. He's a great guy. He doesn't deserve to be hurt. I've made a colossal mess," Ruby said with so much sadness in her eyes.

"Ruby, there has to be a way to break off your engagement with him if you are truly not happy or just going along with it to not be alone," Tiffany said, trying not to give up the information she had learned from Brandon.

Tiffany and Melanie were still shocked that their perspective of their brother was so wrong. They felt guilty for having judged him, and they knew they had to make things right with him as well, without letting him know Brandon spilled the beans on everything.

"I don't know what to do. I know Axl, and I can have a pleasant life together. He is a wonderful man. I invited him to dinner today, and I hope everyone will be nice to him."

"For sure, I will let them know. I'll bring the pasta casserole over to Melanie's tonight. Is Axl allergic to any foods?"

"No, he's not. We are taking the beverages."

"This is turning out to be a great summer, and I know it'll get better once things get sorted out," Tiffany said as she smelled a beautifully ripened mango.

"Can't believe someone harvested mangoes up here," Ruby said as she, too, grabbed a mango.

"I'll get some for the Inn and some for me. I can't wait to

make a tropical fruit salad with these delicious mangoes. Speaking of tropical, my mom and Thomas are going on a romantic getaway. My mom wants a cozy beach resort, but being in the mountains, I'm not sure where to recommend they go."

"What about Hawaii?"

"Mom doesn't like long flights."

"Ok, what about Puerto Rico? I've heard it's an exquisite and romantic place."

"That's not a bad idea. I'll look into resorts there."

"Some other options on the East Coast would be Bermuda, Savannah, Miami, Myrtle Beach…." Ruby trailed off as she noticed Michael was across the street buying coffee with Brandon, who was still in town.

Noticing Ruby's steady gaze, Tiffany noticed she was staring at Michael. You could tell she was in love with him and was fighting the urge to admit it to herself and others.

"So… earth to Ruby."

"Oh, sorry, yes, so there are plenty of options for them if they don't want to fly."

"Yeah, so how about we get all the things we need, then drop them off at the Inn and my place, and then we go for lunch at Willow Acres?"

"Sounds good to me."

The girls continued to shop and found some homemade mango preserves as well from the same vendor. The guests at the Inn were in for a special treat starting tomorrow with the mangoes they found.

* * *

MELANIE CAME OVER to visit Mary Elle at Willow Acres with Ryder. Ryder had woken up with a fever but was feeling better now. She was hoping to get some editing done from her last engagement shoot. She wanted to work till the very end of her pregnancy as she'd done with Ryder, but this time, everything was much harder.

"Maw Maw," Ryder said loudly in delight when he saw Mary Elle in her office. She had been working on a new project.

"Ryder! My boy!" Mary Elle said as she got up to hold him.

"Hi, mom, we came to visit you."

"Hi beautiful, you are glowing," Mary Elle said as she rubbed Melanie's belly.

"Thanks, this pregnancy is a little different from with Ryder. I feel like I blew up overnight," Melanie said, giggling.

"Yes, things after the first pregnancy can be different. I remember when I was pregnant with you. I got nauseous every day and couldn't see or smell the spaghetti. With Tiffany, I didn't get any nausea, but I was always sleepy."

"How was it with Michael?"

"With him, it was a dream. I didn't start showing until I was about eight months along and craved only fruits," Mary Elle said, reminiscing.

"All three pregnancies were quite different. I feel like this time; I am more prepared. I'm so excited. Cade is over the moon, and he caters to the baby and me. Ryder touches my belly and says hello. The last time he did it, the baby jumped as if it was saying hello back."

"That's so beautiful. You should do a diary or baby book and write down the experience. I regret not doing that for you kids."

"That's an amazing idea. I'll have to do that because I didn't do one for Ryder, either."

"When are you going for the ultrasound?"

"I'm postponing it until you get back. This time we knew the baby's gender right away."

"Good. Either way, it's a blessing from God."

"Yes, I know that, and I can't wait to hold my baby and give it as much love. I know Ryder is ready to be a big brother," Melanie said as she caressed Ryder's cheek and placed a kiss on his head.

"He's such a great kid. He's very kind and loving."

"I know. He gets it from his maw maw."

"Have you spoken with Michael?"

"Not today. I forgot to mention that the last time we were all together, I noticed Michael was excited and having fun without alcohol. Tiffany and I also spoke with Brandon, and we found out that Michael has been in love with Ruby since he was in college. Brandon also said that Michael isn't the way he's portrayed himself. He hasn't been dating around, as he has said. In fact, Michael has always stated the opposite. He never wanted to be like dad but thought it would be a good idea to act and pretend to be this Casanova so dad wouldn't think badly of him. Samantha seduced him and led him on to carry out her revenge against dad. Tiffany and I feel terrible, and we need to make amends with Michael, but we don't want him to know that Brandon told us everything about his love for Ruby or his love life."

"I knew my boy wasn't like Bill. I just knew it. What I never expected was for him and Ruby to date secretly. I think deep down I've always known they would end up together, and I just didn't know when or how."

"Now Ruby's in a bind. She's also in love with Michael, but she's scared that he's just going through a rebound phase, and she's already engaged to Axl. Ruby isn't in love with Axl. She said that she doesn't want to be alone."

"That's not a good reason to get engaged. I hope Michael and Ruby find their way back to each other. I don't want to get involved. Matters of the heart should be resolved by those in the relationship. I wish Michael would see that he's loved by so many. I worry about him, but I know God will lead him out of this darkness and into the light and love that he needs."

"I just don't want anyone getting hurt. Tonight, we are meeting at my house for dinner and to hang out. It felt so good to hang out back in the day and just have fun and laugh. I think we all needed that after so much drama has happened. I haven't spoken to dad recently, but I know he's ok. Barb has posted on her social media some photos, and he's looking better, and he's recovering nicely."

"I can't lie. Learning about his secret affair with Samantha was a harsh blow, but I'm grateful that he's no longer my husband. I do hope and pray that he'll be good with Barbara. No matter how much we dislike each other, a wife doesn't deserve her man to walk out on her."

"That's very true. You are such an amazing mom. You are my hero. I don't know what I would have done if that had happened to me. I don't think I would be strong enough to move past it or to forgive them."

"It's by the grace of God. It's his strength; it's his forgiveness. I just give it up to him, and he does the rest."

CHAPTER 10

"Rita, these new pieces are beautiful!" DeeAnn exclaimed as she examined a new clay necklace Rita had just put on display.

"I've been feeling so inspired lately that I haven't stopped making jewelry all week!" Rita said, smiling proudly.

"I think these earrings will be perfect for my trip," Mary Elle said as she studied herself in front of the mirror and brought a pair of colorful earrings up to her face.

"Have you decided where to go?" Rita asked.

"We're thinking something tropical. A cute beach cabana..." Mary Elle said, getting lost in her daydreams.

"What about Tortuga Cove?" DeeAnn asked.

"Where is that? Sounds exotic!" Mary Elle said, turning her full attention over to her sister.

"It's a small island right off of Florida. A friend of mine visited there, and she said she felt like she was in Bora Bora."

Mary Elle grabbed her phone out of her purse and quickly searched the internet for Tortuga Cove. It looked like just the place for her and Thomas to get some much-needed alone time.

"You should go there, Mary Elle. You and Thomas deserve some alone time after everything you've been through."

"I can't wait to tell Thomas about Tortuga Cove. I was worried he'd say no, but he was very open to the idea."

"Thomas is a good man," Rita said.

"He really is," Mary Elle said, smiling brightly as she studied another one of Rita's new pieces.

"How is Bob? I haven't seen him around much," DeeAnn said, leaning against the counter.

"He's doing well. He's in Atlanta now. Mandy is back from studying abroad, and he is helping her move to a new apartment."

"So soon? I thought she was staying there for a year?" Mary Elle asked, concerned.

"Amanda said she didn't like it. She missed her friends too much."

"The food there is delicious! One of my most memorable trips was when I took off to Germany for a summer without a plan," DeeAnn said with a giggle.

DeeAnn had always been the wild one between the three of them. She'd experienced and traveled much more than anyone else Mary Elle knew. Now in her forties, DeeAnn was finally ready to settle down, and Willow Heights was the perfect spot for that.

"Have you and Paul discussed kids?" Mary Elle asked, remembering a recent conversation with DeeAnn about adopting.

"I haven't brought it up..." DeeAnn said, looking around uneasily.

"Why not? You and Paul would make great parents," Rita chimed in.

"We're not married, and I don't know if marriage is on the table."

"Dee, Paul didn't sell his home and all his belongings if he was not thinking about marriage with you," Mary Elle said gently.

"He hasn't ever brought it up, and I don't want to be the one to do it."

Mary Elle and Rita exchanged a look.

"Don't do that. I'm right here," DeeAnn said, rolling her eyes.

"You're being ridiculous. Paul loves you, and I know for a fact he wants to marry you."

"Did he tell you that?" DeeAnn asked, placing a hand on her hip.

"He didn't have to! It's written all over his face."

"I'm going to go with Mary Elle on this one," Rita said as the door chimed, indicating a new arrival.

"Hello, everyone," Sienna said as she walked in.

"You look stunning!" Mary Elle said, noticing that Sienna was doing something different with her hair and was wearing more makeup than usual.

"Thank you," Sienna said shyly as a blush crept onto her cheeks.

"Sienna has been promoted," Rita said proudly.

"Congratulations!" DeeAnn said.

"Thank you. The Nurse Practitioner moved away, and I am taking her spot. Finally, putting my master's degree to use."

The ladies spent the rest of the afternoon catching up and making plans for the future. Mary Elle quickly called Thomas and told him about Tortuga Cove. He gave her the go-ahead, and with the help of Rita and DeeAnn, she booked flights and a hotel. She couldn't wait to get away with the love of her life.

* * *

Cade had rushed Melanie to Doctor Bank's office because she'd been sick all day. It was worse than her usual morning sickness, and he was worried something was wrong. Her sonogram appointment wasn't scheduled until two weeks from today, but Cade requested an emergency sonogram to ensure everything was okay.

"How are you feeling?" Doctor Banks asked Melanie as she looked over Melanie's medical file.

"I'm feeling good. A little nervous, though," Melanie said as she glanced over at Cade.

The sonographer had stepped out of the room and said she had to get Doctor Banks in the middle of doing the sonogram. That had done no favors on Melanie's nerves.

"I thought you might be, but relax. I think you might be happy with what I'm about to tell you."

Cade took Melanie's hand and squeezed it. She was so grateful to have him here and that he missed none of the appointments.

"What is it?" Melanie asked.

"You're having twins!" Doctor Banks said with a laugh.

"Twins?" Melanie and Cade said in unison.

"That's right," Doctor Banks said as she congratulated them.

Melanie couldn't even make out what Doctor Banks was saying. She was still stuck on the twin's part. How were they going to handle three kids? Cade put an arm around Melanie and hugged her, and whispered that he loved her. She was still shocked and couldn't get her brain to work to say she loved Cade. The only thing she could do was smile at him.

On their drive home, Melanie broke down and cried. Cade pulled the car to the side of the road and asked her what was wrong.

"We're having twins," she sobbed.

"Yes, we are," he said as he moved her hair away from her face.

"How...how are we going to handle this?" Melanie asked, searching for answers in his eyes.

"The way we handle everything: together and with help from our families," Cade said, pressing his lips to her forehead.

Melanie knew he was right. These babies were a blessing, and they would only bring them closer together, and they would only fill their home with more love and joy.

"I couldn't do this without you," she said.

"You don't have to," he said before getting the car back on the road.

Melanie looked out the window and thought of all the times she'd prayed for a moment like this. All the time, she'd prayed for a love like the one she shared with Cade. All the times she'd prayed for little babies to raise and love. This was everything she had prayed for, and with the help of those around her and God on her side, they could handle anything life threw at them.

As soon as they got home, they reached out to their families to tell them about the big news.

"We are having twins!" Melanie said, filled with so much happiness and bliss.

"Oh, my goodness! Congratulations!" Mary Elle and Thomas both said on speakerphone.

"I'm so scared but excited simultaneously," Melanie confessed as tears of joy filled her eyes.

"Oh honey, everything is as it should be. You know you can count on us to help you out!" Mary Elle reassured Melanie.

"Thanks, mom," Melanie said as Cade hugged her and placed a hand over her belly.

"See, you don't have to stress about anything. We are all

here to help you," Cade whispered in her ear. Hearing his words caused butterflies to swarm inside her stomach. She was still so in love with him.

After hanging up with Mary Elle and Thomas, they called Cade's parents. They, too, were elated with the news, and it turns out the twins run in Cade's side of the family from his father's side. They, too, offered to help with the babies and couldn't wait to meet them.

"Hi Mel, how's it going?" Tiffany answered her call.

"Well, I have big news to share with you. We are having twins!"

"Are you serious?"

"Yes, I know, it's crazy!"

"Remember that dream I had about you having twins?"

"Yeah, but that was when I was pregnant with Ryder."

"But I called it!"

"Ok, ok, you called it," Melanie said, laughing.

"Have you told dad?"

"Not yet. I need to tell him, Michael, Ruby, and Britney."

"Ok, well, go and spread your good news with them," Tiffany said as she ended the call and said she would text David, letting him know what was happening.

Cade had already texted David and the rest of the Willow Acres gang to let them know the great news.

"Britney! I've missed you so much," Melanie said as she answered Britney's facetime call.

"You seem exceptionally happy today. What's going on?"

"I have amazing news. We are having twins!"

"I can't believe it; it's like Tiffany's dream!" Britney said as she, too, remembered that dream.

"I guess, in a way. It's so random that you called me when I was thinking of you just now. You were the next person I was going to call to tell the great news," Melanie said, realizing the synchronicity.

"I was calling to let you know I am planning on visiting you and wanted to make sure you'd be ok with that. I miss Willow Heights," Britney said as she pouted.

"I'm sure you mean you miss Jasper," Melanie jokingly replied.

"I miss him. I haven't connected with him in some weeks. Things got hectic here with work and traveling."

"I know it will thrill him to see you. I probably shouldn't mention it, but he's head over heels for you."

"Oh, stop it. He's such a nice guy. I don't deserve him."

"Don't be silly. You should really change your mind about that."

"Who knows, maybe he can tame me?" Britney said teasingly.

"Well, I can't wait to see you and spend time with you."

"Me too. How's Michael doing?"

"He's better. He just needs time to refocus and rediscover himself."

"Yeah, maybe he can take a solo trip somewhere. It's very healing."

"Maybe. I have a feeling that things will change for him soon. Tiffany and I are discovering who he really is as well. We've made the mistake of judging him instead of loving him."

"We all make mistakes like that, just fix things and don't become estranged."

"How's your mom?"

"Things are progressing. We keep in contact more often; I've come to terms with many things and forgiven her. It's a day-to-day situation."

"I know it's difficult, but I commend you for not giving up and working at it."

"You got it. I have to go now; I have a flight to catch early in the morning but wanted to talk to you. Say hi to Cade and Ryder for me, please. Love ya."

"Love you too, Brit."

Melanie and Britney were great friends, and no matter the distance, their friendship stood the test of time and space.

Melanie wanted to share the joyous news about the twins with her father but didn't know if she was ready to speak with him again. She had been concerned about his health and had spoken to him a few times. He'd also visited Willow Heights and volunteered at David's sanctuary, but she didn't think things between them would ever be the way they should be.

"Here goes nothing…." Melanie said quietly as she grabbed her cellphone to dial her father's number.

"I'm sure he will be happy to hear the good news," Cade said, showing his support for her decision to tell Bill.

"You're right. I shouldn't hold grudges."

"Hello?" Bill answered.

"Hi Dad, how are you?"

"I'm great, Mel. How are you, Cade and Ryder?"

"We are all doing well. I was calling to share some great news. Cade and I are having twins."

"Oh really? That's great. I guess it's from my grandmother's side. She had two sets of twins. My uncles and aunts never thought the twin gene would come down this far since my father nor his siblings had any twins, and neither did I."

"Really? I didn't know there were twins in our family as well."

"Yes, there are. I guess I never got around to discussing my family much. Listen, Mel, I've been thinking, and I know I've failed as a father. I've meant to get together with you, Michael, and Tiffany to talk. I have a lot to say, and having this near-death experience has really made me reconsider every decision I've made as a father and husband," Bill said in a sincere tone.

"Dad, don't worry. I don't want you stressing over anything. We will get together soon and talk things through. Just know that we all love you," Melanie said, knowing that life is precious, and one day we're here, the next, we're gone.

"Thanks, darling. I do hope we can meet soon, and congratulations on the twins. What a marvelous blessing God has given you," Bill said with a crack in his voice.

Melanie knew God had been working on Bill's heart and bringing to mind many things that needed to be healed within himself and their family. It just felt like each time they made progress, something else would come out, and everything would fall apart all over again. She hoped that the last surprise really was the last one.

CHAPTER 11

"Let's make this night a good one, okay guys?" Tiffany said to the group as they waited for Ruby and Axl to join them.

"We promise to be on our best behavior," Brandon said with a snicker.

"I'm serious. Axl's been nothing but nice to all of us," Tiffany said, sounding more like her mom than she would like.

Just then, the doorbell rang, and Tiffany gave everyone one last stern look before getting the door.

"Welcome! We're so happy to have you here, Axl," Tiffany said.

"Thank you for having me," Axl said with a genuine smile.

"Any friend of Ruby's is a friend of ours," Michael said and clapped Axl on the back.

Tiffany rolled her eyes at him. He sounded so fake, but at least he was trying.

"It smells delicious," Ruby said as she joined Melanie in the kitchen.

"I just heated a frozen lasagna," Melanie said with a guilty smile.

"I'm sure it'll be great," Ruby said as she pulled her into a hug and congratulated her on the twins.

"Soon, that'll be us," Axl said as he placed an arm around Ruby and pulled her close.

Tiffany couldn't help but notice how Ruby tensed up. She knew she should mind her business, but she really wanted Ruby to end things with Axl. Not only because of Michael but because Ruby deserved to experience true love.

"Let's find our seats. I placed name cards on the table," Melanie said.

Melanie had seated Michael across from Ruby, hoping to get them talking. Tiffany hadn't thought it was a good idea to be meddling, but Melanie didn't listen. The group dove into the salad, lasagna, and garlic bread. They enjoyed a nice glass of wine and got to know Axl better. Tiffany was happy to note that everyone had kept their promise and was nice to Axl. There was no denying he was in love with Ruby, not that you could blame him. Ruby was beautiful and kind. She was smart and gracious. She was everything that any man could ever want in a wife. Tiffany watched as Axl whispered something to Ruby, making her blush. Tiffany turned her gaze to Michael and saw his jaw clench.

"So, Axl, where do you work again? Target?" Michael asked with a snicker.

He was joking about the red polo shirt and khaki pants Axl was wearing. Tiffany kicked him under the table, but her brother didn't seem to get the hint.

"Actually, I'm a Real Estate Acquisition Analyst for a development firm similar to the one you got fired from."

Suddenly, the room fell quiet, and the tension in the air was palpable. Michael stood and walked out of the house without saying a word. Ruby quickly stood and ran after him.

"I'm so sorry, Axl. Michael's been going through a lot lately," Tiffany said, trying to tame the situation.

"It's fine," he said as he glared at the door, Ruby had just walked out of.

"Would you like some more food?" Melanie asked him.

"No, thank you. Everything was delicious. Thank you for having me over," Axl said as he excused himself and went after Ruby.

* * *

"MICHAEL?" Ruby asked as she approached him. His back was to her.

"I'm sorry about what I said to Axl. I just want to be alone."

"I think we should talk," Ruby said.

"There's nothing for us to talk about," Michael said, turning to face her.

"I think there is..."

"Ruby, whatever you do with your life is none of my business," Michael said.

That simple statement cut through to her. She wanted to be strong, but she hated feeling this way. She was tired of being confused and sad all the time. Tired of feeling like she was making a mistake.

"Do you really mean that?" Ruby asked, looking straight into his eyes.

Michael looked up at the sky and began to pace.

"Talk to me, Michael."

He stopped pacing and came to a stop in front of her.

"I want to be selfish and you not to marry him. Pick me,

Ruby. But I can't. What if I turn out to be like him? What if I hurt you? I don't deserve you, Ruby..."

"You're nothing like him. I know you, Michael. The real you."

Michael said nothing. He walked over to the gazebo Cade had built for Melanie and took a seat on the bench. Ruby followed him and took a seat next to him.

"All your life, you've blamed yourself for what your father did. You've blamed yourself for not telling your mother, but you were just a kid."

"I should have said something..."

"You were a child, and your father made you promise not to. No one blames you, Michael. You need to forgive yourself. We all love you, and we want what's best for you. Look at what keeping all of this inside has done to you."

They jumped apart when they heard the crunching of leaves on the ground. Axl appeared in the gazebo a few seconds later.

"Everything alright out here?" he asked them.

"Everything is fine," Ruby said as she walked over to him.

Axl turned and guided her back to Melanie's house. Ruby turned to look at Michael one last time. Her heart ached for him, and she wished more than anything that he would finally forgive himself. He needed to do that to be free. Michael had been beating himself up over his father's mistakes since he learned about the affairs. Ruby remembered finding him under the school's bleachers in tears. He'd confided in her then, and she'd never seen him so broken. Michael had always been known to be happy-go-lucky. He was a star athlete and the top student in his class. After that day under the bleachers, everything changed. No one knew why his attitude was so different. He got into fights in school, and he isolated himself from friends. He was never happy anymore, and he held himself back from enjoying life. Michael convinced himself he didn't deserve happiness.

After Ruby and Axl went inside, Cade appeared and walked to Michael.

"Hey, how's everything?" Cade asked.

"I'm here. Sorry about my behavior earlier. I didn't mean to ruin the night."

"It's ok. I know you're dealing with a lot. I wanted to get some fresh air as well."

"How did you do it?" Michael asked Cade suddenly.

"Do what?" Cade asked, unsure of what Michael was asking.

"You know when Melanie was still trying to work things out with Everett, and you were in love with her? How did you control yourself?"

"Oh, well, it was difficult. I wanted to tell her I loved her, but she was still healing from her breakup. She was also pregnant, and I didn't want to cause too much stress on her. But one thing is for sure; it was my love for her that kept me from pounding Everett's face. I couldn't stand that pretentious jerk. If you love Ruby as much as you think, let her know how you feel and let her decide what she wants. It's clear as day that she's not in love with him. She practically winced at the thought of having his baby."

"Yeah, I noticed that too, but didn't know if I had imagined it," Michael said with a smile.

"If you love her, tell her. If she doesn't want to hear it, then show her. Go after her. She's not married yet. There's still time to change the path you are on."

"Thanks for the advice."

Both Michael and Cade walked back inside the house. Things had cooled off, and Ruby had now distanced herself from Axl by hanging out with the girls.

"Sorry about earlier. I hope the night isn't ruined on my account," Michael said to Axl.

"We are cool. Don't worry about it," Axl said in a nonchalant tone.

"Tiffany decided we will play charades, girls versus boys," David said as he took a sip of his beer.

"Great," Michael said as he rolled his eyes. Tiffany, Ruby, and Melanie always won because they were so in sync with each other.

"Let the game begin," Melanie announced excitedly.

As predicted by Michael, the girls won, and they had no shame in rubbing it in their faces. The night turned out to not be so bad after all. Michael was happy because he'd caught Ruby staring at him a few times. She wouldn't be doing that if she didn't still have feelings for him. He just needed to trust God, like his mom always told him to. If it were meant to be, Ruby would come back to him.

CHAPTER 12

"So, they're thinking of opening a branch in London. I might head the team over there," Axl was saying as he and Ruby were having breakfast at the Busy Bee Coffee Shop. Axl was having fried eggs, hash browns, and sausage. While Ruby opted for scrambled eggs with toast and a glass of orange juice.

"Does that mean you'll have to move to London?" Ruby asked.

"That means you and I will move to London," Axl said with a smile.

Ruby felt her heart stop at the thought of being so far away from everyone she loved.

"It'll most likely happen after our wedding," Axl said, filling the silence.

Ruby smiled at Axl and took a drink from her orange juice. Her throat was suddenly dry, and she had lost her appetite. She enjoyed Axl's company, and she knew he would be a great husband. Ruby just didn't feel how you should feel about the person you would be spending the rest of your life with. She tried to fall in love with him. She tried giving herself completely to him. Ruby had even distanced herself from Michael and anyone that might affect her feelings for Axl, but nothing had worked.

The door to the front of the coffee shop opened, and Michael stepped in with Brandon. She felt her heart speed up, and her mood instantly lifted. They walked to the counter and placed their order, not noticing Ruby or Axl.

"Ruby?" Axl said, bringing her attention back to their table.

"Yes?" she asked.

"What's going on?" Axl asked in a hushed tone.

"What do you mean?" Ruby asked, trying to focus her attention on him.

"I'm not a fool, Ruby. I see the way you look at him, the way you light up around him. What's going on between you and Michael?"

"Nothing. We're just friends," Ruby said as she organized the sugar packets on their table.

Out of the corner of her eye, she could see Michael and Brandon walking towards the door with their orders. She looked up, and her eyes locked with Michaels. He smiled at her, and she couldn't help but smile back. Axl sighed, and Ruby looked back at him. She felt guilty that he'd just witnessed that.

"Ruby, I think you're a wonderful girl. I just don't think you're the girl for me," Axl said.

"What are you saying?"

"I think we should end things before we both regret this."

Ruby knew what he was saying was true, but she couldn't help feeling sad. She didn't know the future or if she'd ever meet anyone like Axl again.

"I'm so sorry, Axl..." Ruby said.

"There's nothing to be sorry about. We gave it our best

shot. I'll always remember our time together and wish you the best in everything that you do," Axl said as he stood.

He kissed Ruby's forehead and began to say something, but then shook his head and walked away. A wave of sadness overcame Ruby, and she felt more alone now than before. She knew being with Axl wasn't ideal, but at least she had someone. Someone that loved her and cherished her. She didn't want to be alone anymore. All her friends were married and having kids while she was still single because she'd spent most of her life pining over someone that never felt the same about her.

"Axl, wait!" Ruby said just as he was about to walk out.

Axl turned and looked at her, confused. Ruby stared at him for a moment, unsure of what to say. They stepped outside to let a couple into the coffee shop.

"Maybe we can work this out," Ruby said once they were outside.

"Ruby... I've thought this over for a long time. I've always felt like something was holding you back. Something kept you from loving me fully, and I could never understand why things felt that way. Now that I've seen you with Michael, I know why. Ruby, you'll never love me the way you love him."

"You don't know that."

"Are you willing to let Michael go forever?"

Ruby took a moment to think it over. Was she willing to never speak to Michael again? What would her life be like without him? She'd never imagined a life without him before, and she wasn't sure how she felt about this. A noise across the street drew her attention away, and she spotted Michael and Brandon leaving Rita's store. She looked back at Axl, and her heart broke once again. This was the toughest decision she ever had to make. No matter what she did, someone was going to get hurt.

* * *

Axl's last words kept replaying in her mind, "It's for the best, Ruby. I can't keep doing this. Watching you torn as well. It's not fair for both of us."

Ruby knew he was right. She was torn. Deep down inside, she knew she had to face whatever was coming. Loneliness was her biggest nemesis. Ruby went back inside the Busy Bee Coffee and paid for their breakfast. She texted Tiffany and told her that Axl had ended things.

Without hesitation, Tiffany asked Ruby to go over to the Inn so they could talk. Tiffany was the only on-site manager today and couldn't leave the Inn unattended.

"Ruby, so glad you made it," Tiffany said as she greeted her with a hug.

"I don't know how I'm feeling. I'm relieved, yet I'm sad and confused. This was the right thing to do for both of us, but I feel horrible that Axl is heartbroken as well," Ruby sobbed as they walked to the garden area near the pool.

"Oh, Ruby, I know it's tough right now because you are going through the motions, but trust me, this was the best for you both. I'm sure Axl will find someone new and be happy, and so will you."

"I don't know, Tiff; it seems like things can't be fixed between Michael and me. He broke my heart, and I ruined our friendship. I thought when we began dating that it was meant to be, but then Samantha came along, and everything changed. It broke my heart into a million pieces. I had to watch as the man I had loved and cared for just walked out on me and didn't even care enough to properly break up with me," Ruby continued, sobbing.

"I don't blame you for being cautious this time around, but you don't know really know the real Michael. I'm afraid none of us knew him truly. We spoke with Brandon, and he told us the truth about everything. Brandon said that Michael wasn't the promiscuous man we thought he was. In fact, he lied about casually dating all those women so our father wouldn't judge him because he wasn't a womanizer like him. It was all a lie. Michael only broke things off with you because he thought he didn't deserve you. He thought that by marrying Samantha, you would forget him and move on to someone better."

"I had no idea. I thought it was all true because I saw how the girls would fight for his attention. He was the top athlete, charming and so handsome. I assumed all the girls wanted to be with him as much as I did."

"That might be true, but Michael never felt like any of them were for him. At least that's what Brandon has told us. Michael has only really cared about you," Tiffany said as she handed Ruby some facial tissue to wipe away her tears.

"I wish I would've known all of this before…."

"I'm not saying that you have to apologize to him because honestly, he did mess up big time, and he needs to recognize his mistakes and make amends. What I'm saying is that it's time you both talked things out. I think reconnecting and establishing your friendship is crucial right now. Hang out, have fun, talk, do what friends do, and see where it goes from there."

"I would forgive him if he apologized, but I don't think I'm ready to just give my heart to him again. It'll take time," Ruby said with a small smile and a glimmer of hope in her eyes.

"Life is too precious to hold yourself back from true happiness. I want the best for both of you. You both deserve to be happy and to find love."

"Thanks for listening and being here with me, Tiffany. We've known each other since we were kids, and you've been my best friend all this time. I know I snuck around and kept this from you, and, for that, I'm sorry. I know this has affected our friendship and trust as well. Please forgive me for lying and not being completely honest with you. I love you and don't want to ruin our friendship, either."

"Don't worry about it. I understand you only lied because you knew I was overprotective of you, even though Michael is my brother, and we didn't know he was lying about dating random women. I'm sorry too because I was angry and didn't tell you, and I know I could have been more supportive." Tiffany said as she hugged Ruby again and told her she loved her, too.

CHAPTER 13

"Good morning, big bro," Melanie said as she walked into Michael's room and opened the blinds. Mary Elle and Thomas left on their beach getaway, and Melanie was left in charge of watching over her brother. Brandon left for California, and it seemed like Michael was falling into another slump. Michael groaned and rolled onto his side.

Melanie walked over to the other side of the bed and joined him. She needed to elevate her feet because she currently had no ankles. Her feet were very swollen and hurting.

"What's going on?" she asked him.

"Trying to sleep," he said.

"What's really going on?" Melanie asked, not ready to let him off the hook.

"Nothing."

"Ruby and Axl broke up," Melanie said, hoping to get a reaction out of him.

"Why?" Michael asked, surprising Melanie because he seemed upset.

"She didn't love him..." Melanie said, still confused by his reaction.

"She needs to marry him. She can learn to love him. Axl is good for her. He deserves her," Michael said, sitting up in bed.

"And you don't?" Melanie asked.

"No, I don't. Everyone knows that, Mel. How could you let her do this?"

"I didn't let her do anything. She is a grown woman that can make her own decisions. She deserves to be happy and to know true love. So do you, Michael. Why are you holding yourself back, and why do you think you don't deserve her?"

"I'm just like him, aren't I? I'll only hurt her and prove to everyone that they were right about me."

"If you were anything like Dad, you wouldn't care if you hurt her or not."

"I heard you and Tiffany talking about us during the camping trip. Tiffany was upset that you'd even think of Ruby and I dating."

"Tiffany didn't mean it."

"Yes, she did."

"Well, she's wrong. We didn't know you truly cared for her. I know you do. Otherwise, you wouldn't be like this. I know you're not sad about losing Samantha. You didn't love her, it was just lust, and I know it's not about dad. He didn't cheat on you, it was on mom, and she's basically over it. She's not letting his secret affairs ruin her life or take her joy away. She's out there living her best life with the love of her life. Don't you see? We all deserve to be loved and happy, even you, Michael. No matter how much you think you are, you are not like dad. You are more like mom. You love and expect nothing in return. You are kind and caring and a great friend. Don't let your poor decisions ruin the rest of your life."

"I hurt her, and I don't know how to fix it. She hates me, and she's right to do so."

"Michael, she doesn't hate you. She's hurt because of how things ended and transpired, but she doesn't hate you. If she did, would she smile when you walked into the room? No, she wouldn't. You mean so much to her. It's clear to all of us. Don't be a fool."

"That's what Brandon told me. Cade also told me to go after her."

"Cade, said that?"

"Yeah, we had a bonding moment. I have to say; he's a pretty cool dude."

"He's adorable," Melanie gushed; you could tell she was crazy for Cade.

"I can't believe they broke up," Michael said with a slight smile.

"Well, it would not work out, anyway. She's in love with someone else."

"This little pep talk has elevated my mood. I think I'll get up, have breakfast, and shower," Michael said as he headed out of the bedroom.

"I'll be here, resting...."

Melanie couldn't help but text Cade a quick 'I love you' message. She had been blessed beyond her wildest dreams. God had answered yet another one of her prayers. She had always wanted Michael and Cade to bond, but they were so different from each other. God works in mysterious ways.

Mary Elle and Thomas had entrusted a special task to Melanie and Tiffany. She had planned a small graduation party for Lorraine because she passed her G.E.D test and wanted to make her feel special. Lorraine and Wyatt had become part of their family and were loved dearly by Mary Elle and Thomas. Lorraine was like a daughter, and Wyatt was like a grandson to them. The girls had decided to trick

Lorraine and Wyatt by inviting them over for a home welcoming party for Mary Elle and Thomas but little did they know it was a surprise graduation party instead. It was all arranged, and Mary Elle and Thomas would arrive the day before and be there to surprise them.

* * *

"I LOVE WATCHING the sun go down here," Tiffany said as she laid back on the blanket she had set up earlier.

She surprised David with dinner at the sanctuary since he'd worked so hard between his day job at Willow Acres and nights at the sanctuary. She prepared a Mediterranean orzo pasta salad that he loved. Tiffany wasn't the most skilled in the kitchen, but she had found a newfound interest in cooking. Many things that hadn't interested her before were suddenly piquing her interest.

"I'm glad you said that because there's something I've been wanting to tell you..." David said in an excited tone.

"Oh yeah? What is it?" Tiffany said, interested in what he had to say.

"I took Mr. Gallows up on his offer. That land you see over there... that's ours now."

"David, that's fantastic! What are you planning on doing with it?" Tiffany asked, trying not to freak out that he said "ours," not just his.

"I thought we could build a house where we could raise our kids and have our little family."

Tiffany's face broke out into a wide grin. She'd never been so in love or felt so loved as she did with David. She didn't think she would ever want to have kids or to settle down and make a home, but the more in love she fell with David, the more those things started pulling at her heartstrings.

"I would love that," she said as she leaned in and kissed him.

"I had wanted to tell you for some time, but I wasn't sure how you would react."

"Why?"

"Oh, you know, because you're an independent woman, and you don't need a man or kids," David said in a playful tone.

"Maybe this independent woman has decided that she would like a future with her prince charming after all."

"Well, in that case... Tiffany, would you make me the happiest man and accept to help me move some things into the new land?" David said, laughing as he saw Tiffany's jaw drop, thinking he was proposing to her.

"That's not funny, David!" Tiffany said, realizing he had tricked her and that he was just teasing her.

"Oh, come on, did you really think I was going to propose like this?"

"Yes, actually I did!"

"Well, you don't know how I will propose or when, but believe me, it'll be phenomenal, and you'll never forget it," David said as he leaned close and gave her a sweet kiss on the lips.

Tiffany was reeling from all the emotions she was feeling. This summer had truly become an amazing one unexpectedly. She couldn't wait for the moment when David would ask for her hand in marriage.

* * *

MICHAEL AND WYATT were also bonding and enjoyed hanging out recently, and they had been watching an anime series about a boy that was a ninja. Melanie tried watching with them, but she just couldn't get into it. They said it was a great anime series that showed how hard work and persistence helped develop the young boy's character and earned respect from others in his village that disliked him and thought less of him.

Melanie and Tiffany eagerly worked to find all the flowers and balloons they would need for Lorraine's surprise party, which was just a few days away. Wyatt had visited and spent the night at Lorraine's house, which worked out perfectly and gave them time to clean, set up, and decorate and Mary Elle and Thomas time to get home without being seen by them. They parked Thomas' truck in the garage, with no one suspecting they were home already.

"Welcome home! We missed you!" the girls said as Mary Elle and Thomas walked into the kitchen through the garage door.

"We missed you too!" Mary Elle said as she ran to hug them.

"Wow, nice tan, Thomas," Tiffany said as he walked in with their rolling luggage.

"Thanks! I have to admit; that I had a great time. Mary Elle knew we needed this vacation, and it was amazing. Where's Michael?" Thomas asked as he looked around.

"He's upstairs. He doesn't know you were arriving today," Tiffany replied as she continued to group balloons together to make an arch.

"Everything is looking great! I can't wait to surprise Lorraine. She's worked so hard to achieve her dream," Mary Elle said as she dropped her purse on the kitchen counter and started to help Melanie with some of the flowers.

"Thanks, mom," Melanie said, almost out of breath. Her belly had grown since Mary Elle last saw her.

"You are radiant. Motherhood has really done you good," Mary Elle said as she planted a kiss on her head.

"Food has been ordered and delivered tomorrow afternoon," Tiffany told her.

"Where's Wyatt?" Thomas asked as he came back downstairs to help the ladies decorate.

"He went over to Lorraine's and stayed the night. He will be back tomorrow."

"Everything worked out. This is going to be a great party," Thomas said, smiling.

CHAPTER 14

"Don't you have the sweetest older sister, Penny?" Rita asked her little corgi as she ran to her little round bed in the corner of the living room with a toy Sienna had just gifted her.

Penny had a small bed in almost all the rooms of the house. She was a spoiled little dog.

"She's adorable," Sienna said as she watched the dog struggling to get the toy onto the bed.

"She sure is. I made your favorite macaroni and cheese casserole for dinner," Rita told her.

"With the pieces of ham?" Sienna asked as her stomach grumbled.

"Rita!" Bob called out from the kitchen.

"We're in the living room, honey," Rita said loud enough for Bob to hear her.

"Rita, you have to see this," Bob said, holding out an envelope that looked like it'd seen better days.

Rita took the envelope from Bob and couldn't believe her eyes when she saw who it was from. The envelope had been forwarded from their previous mailing address. Rita's hands were shaking so much that she was having a hard time opening the envelope.

"Do you want me to do it?" Sienna asked.

Rita couldn't form any words. She nodded and handed the envelope to Sienna. Bob put an arm around Rita and pulled her close. He kissed the top of her head. She looked up at him and smiled. She thought this day would never come and had given up hope for a long time.

Sienna handed the letter to Rita, and she read it.

Rita,

This letter might be too little too late, but I've been thinking of you, Robert, and the kids nonstop. I miss you all. I miss you every day and want nothing more than to come home.

I know that everything I've done is unforgivable and you all probably want nothing to do with me. I understand that completely and if that's the case, I will stay away.

I love you, Rita. I would like to see you and reconnect. Below please find my contact information.

Your sister,

Emma

RITA WIPED the tears off her face and let out a small laugh. Was this really happening?

"She wants to see us, Bob. She's ready to come home," Rita said to him with tears of joy in her eyes.

Bob was crying happy tears as well. He pulled her closer, and they cried in each other's arms. Little by little, God was answering all the desires of their hearts.

"You should call her," Sienna said. "Her number is at the bottom of the page."

Rita quickly grabbed her cellphone and dialed the number on the letter. She gave Sienna a nervous but excited smile.

"Hello?"

"Emma? It's Rita," Rita said as she squeezed Bob's hand.

"Rita! Oh my gosh... when I didn't hear from you, I thought you didn't want anything to do with me because I never heard from you after I sent the letter."

"It was lost in the mail, apparently. We moved to Willow Heights, and it took them this long to forward it to our new address. I can't believe you reached out to us. We have missed you, too. Where are you?"

"I'm in Savannah and wanted to visit you and the family. I've been in rehab, and I have been sober for about a year now. I thought it was best to stay away while I got myself back on track. It's been a long road, but it's been worth it."

"That's amazing. I can't wait for you to visit. I'll get the kids to come and visit as well. It'll be a big family reunion."

"I would love that. I can't wait to see you all and make up for all the years I've been absent," Emma cried.

Sienna was moved to see the bond between her mother and aunt. This also meant that Rita would introduce Sienna to her sister, Emma. All the missing pieces of Rita's family were coming together. Bob was so happy to see that Rita's dream was coming true. They thought that after such a long time without receiving news from Emma, she had somehow passed away. Emma had substance abuse problems and would go on binges. The drug use had caused Emma to lose her kids and her marriage to fall apart. She couldn't keep a job and was living in motels or on the streets. Rita and Bob had always been there for and had adopted her kids so they wouldn't be in foster care or get separated since most people didn't adopt a group of siblings. Rita always hoped that this day would come and that Emma would return and be a part of their lives again.

"Mom, is that my aunt you were talking to?" Sienna asked Rita for clarification.

"Yes, Emma is my sister. She had been estranged, but now she's ready to visit us, and I'm hoping she decides to stay. She's Alexanders, Andrews, and Amanda's mother. Bob and I adopted them when Emma lost custody of them. We feared they would be separated if they were placed in foster care, and that was something we couldn't allow to happen."

"I see. Well, I'm excited to meet her. I'm sure she doesn't know about me," Sienna said with a small smile.

"She knows about you, but she doesn't know we have reconnected and that you now live here with us. You will love her. She's amazing. She's the fun aunt every kid wants to have."

"She sounds amazing," Sienna said as she gave Rita a congratulatory hug.

* * *

THE DAY HAD FINALLY ARRIVED when Lorraine thought they were throwing Mary Elle and Thomas a homecoming party. Everything was ready for the big surprise party.

"Ok, we have everything ready. Food has been delivered, and drinks are served. We should get ready in case Lorraine and Wyatt arrive early," Melanie said as she took a seat on the couch. She was starting to feel exhausted. Being pregnant with twins was not as easy as she thought it would be.

"You're right. Wyatt is always early to all our parties. We should get ready now just in case," Tiffany agreed as she opened the door to find Cade standing at the door, ready to ring the doorbell.

"Cade, you're early," Tiffany said as she greeted him.

"I had a feeling my girl needed to get ready and didn't want her to drive home and then come back," Cade replied as he walked inside and went over to give Melanie a small kiss.

"You're too good," Melanie said as she grabbed the bag, he brought with her clothing and comfy shoes.

"Let me help you up," Cade said as he helped Melanie off the sofa and walked her to the bathroom.

"That's so sweet of you. She was just saying she needed to get ready but was tired. Her back hurts since her belly has gotten so big lately," Tiffany shared.

"I know. I got her some tape to help her carry the weight of the belly. It's a surprise. She had mentioned seeing it on social media and motherhood pages and said she would order some, but she forgot, so I thought I would get it for her."

"Oh, I've seen that tape too. It's very helpful, and moms love it."

"Babe, thanks for the tape! I didn't think you were listening to me when I mentioned it. I really appreciate it," Melanie shouted from the bathroom.

Cade smiled and blushed. He loved his wife so much and knew that carrying twins was taking a toll on her body. It was the least he could do. Tiffany left to get ready and come back with David. Mary Elle and Thomas were putting the finishing touches on the décor and wrapping a special gift for Lorraine. Michael was getting ready upstairs. After talking to Melanie, he was in a better mood. He missed Wyatt. He always wanted a little brother, and now he had one, and he enjoyed playing basketball, watching their favorite anime series, and talking about life. Wyatt had big dreams and was a hardworking young man. Michael believed Wyatt had big things in store and couldn't wait to be there for him.

"Everything looks wonderful!" Mary Elle said as she walked into the room with Thomas following close behind.

"You all did a good job here," Thomas agreed.

"I hope Lorraine will like it. I want her to see that we all support her and want what's best for her," Tiffany said.

Rita, Bob, and Sienna arrived with a casserole and placed it with the rest of the food. The Willow Acres staff joined them, too.

"Long time no see," Omar said as he approached DeeAnn and Paul, "Allow me to introduce you to my wife, Camila."

"Wife?" Paul asked, surprised.

"Yes, we've recently reconnected," Camila said as she glanced at Omar with a loving gaze.

"Welcome to Willow Heights, Camila. My name is DeeAnn, and this is my boyfriend Paul," DeeAnn said, extending her hand out to her.

Camila shook DeeAnn's hand and said, "I am happy to finally make your acquaintance. Omar has spoken highly of you both."

"That's their car pulling up! Everyone, get ready," Mary Elle said, interrupting them.

Everyone turned their attention towards the door. Ten people had confetti cannons ready to go off as soon as Lorraine and Wyatt walked in.

"Congratulations!" Everyone shouted in unison as soon as Lorraine walked in.

Lorraine stood with a hand to her heart as she thanked each of them.

"Congrats, grad," David said, hugging her.

Tiffany gave her a small graduation dog plush that everyone had signed.

"This is so sweet," Lorraine said as she read everyone's sweet messages on the dog.

"This wouldn't be a graduation party without a diploma," Thomas said as he handed Lorraine a framed diploma he created on the computer with David's help. He even got it framed at the town's frame shop.

"You guys...." Lorraine said as she wiped the happy tears from her face.

"You worked so hard, and we are so proud of you," Mary Elle said as she enveloped her in a hug.

"I never thought I could accomplish anything; I am so grateful to you and Thomas for always believing in me and cheering me on, even when I thought it would best to just quit," Lorraine said through happier tears.

Wyatt was still shocked and was just able to smile as he walked into the house. He was so proud of his mother and knew that God had made big changes in her, and this was a prayer that God had answered for him.

"Mary Elle, I didn't have a chance to tell you about all that's been going on, but Emma reached out to me, and we reconnected. She'll be visiting us soon." Rita shared her big news with her best friend.

"That's unbelievable. I'm so happy for you," Mary Elle said as she hugged Rita.

"Congratulations on the twins as well. God blessing all of us so much!"

"He truly is. He's amazing."

The party was a hit, and everyone had a great time. Lorraine felt so much joy and love. She felt like she had also found her family with Mary Elle and her family and friends.

CHAPTER 15

"I'll be arriving this Friday," Britney texted Melanie.

"Can't wait to see you," Melanie replied with a cheerful face.

Melanie counted down the days left until Britney's arrival and prepared her guest room for her. The twins weren't due for a few months, but Melanie was cleaning out Ryder's nursery and had moved him into the guestroom. She was trying not to be anxious about that yet and promised herself to just enjoy her pregnancy and family until the day arrived for the twins to join them. The twins were a hyper bunch and were constantly moving around and kept her up most nights, but she was excited to have one of her best friends over.

"Cade, I think we'll need a bigger house soon," Melanie said as she turned to face Cade, who was lying in bed next to her watching a basketball game.

"Honey, we can make an addition to the house, or we can make part of the basement a guestroom."

"You think that's easier than buying a new house?"

"No, but it's not as expensive," Cade said with a laugh.

The cabin Cade had built was used for short-term rentals and was booked throughout the following year.

"Britney's coming to visit this Friday, and I wanted to prepare the guestroom for her."

"Don't worry; I'll get it ready for her. Just rest."

"Thanks, hon, you're the best."

"I know," Cade said, laughing.

"I spoke with Michael the other day, and he said you and him had bonded; that brought so much joy to my heart."

"Well, I told him the truth when he asked me how I had dealt with seeing you and Everett together when you were still trying to figure things out. I told him I wanted to punch Everett in the face but that my love for you didn't allow me. I loved you too much to bring any additional drama into your life."

"You're too much. I can't believe that's how you really felt?" Melanie said, surprised.

"I felt like that, but you didn't know. No one knew because I kept my cool. I'm Mr. Cool," Cade said, smiling.

* * *

"BILL?" DeeAnn said as she answered the doorbell.

"Hi, DeeAnn. Sorry to show up unannounced. I came to visit the kids," Bill said as he stood with Barb next to him.

"Come in, please."

"Sorry, I don't know Mary Elle's address, and I thought showing up at Willow Acres would be too much."

"It's ok, no problem. Tiffany is at work; Michael is living with Mary Elle, and Thomas and Melanie are also at work."

"Being the weekend, I thought maybe they were here."

"Well, let me call Melanie and ask. She has some weekends off, so you never know."

"Thanks. I wanted to surprise them. That's why we didn't call."

"Ok, I won't tell her you're in town. I'll just ask if she's working."

"Hi Aunt D, how are you?"

"I'm good, and I was just calling to see how you were."

"I'm fine, just exhausted. The babies have been hyper today and don't stop moving around my belly."

"Are you at home today?"

"Yes, I'm at home. My friend Britney is visiting. Did you want to come over?"

"No, darling. I just wanted to know if you were at work, that's all."

"Is everything ok?"

"Yes, just wanted to say hi," DeeAnn said awkwardly.

"Ok, Aunt D. Well, if you need anything, just let me know."

"Will do. Take care."

"That was awkward," Barb snorted.

"Well, at least we now know Melanie's at home. You know her address, right?"

"Yes, we do. Thank you, Dee."

"No problem. It was nice seeing you both."

Bill and Barb left DeeAnn's house and headed to Melanie's. Bill was nervous. He wasn't the same anymore. Ever since his heart attack, he felt weaker and less aggressive. He hoped his kids would give him the time of day and accept his apology, especially Michael.

* * *

"YOUR LIFE IS LIKE A MOVIE," Melanie said with a laugh.

Britney told Melanie and Ruby about her latest trip and how she'd gone bungee jumping with friends. She had the most adventurous life of anyone that they knew. Her life seemed like lots of fun to outsiders, but Melanie knew from what Britney had told her before that it wasn't always greener on the other side. There were many nights when Britney went to sleep with an empty feeling inside. Sometimes she felt like nothing was enough. As soon as she reached one goal, she was already thinking of the next thing. She never stopped just enjoying life.

"I guess you could say that," Britney said as she petted Melanie's cat.

"Does Jasper know you're here?" Ruby asked.

"No, I haven't told him. I feel bad that I stopped answering his calls and texts..."

"Why did you do that?" Melanie asked.

The last time she'd spoken to Britney, she'd been totally smitten with Jasper.

"Honestly? I don't know. I was hanging out with Chase at the music festival, and I felt guilty, so I just thought it was best to avoid him."

"Brit..."

"I know, I know. You don't have to say anything. I messed up, but I'll apologize to him."

There was a knock at the door, and Melanie called out for them to come in.

"It must be Tiffany and Michael. I invited them over today," Melanie said, hoping Ruby wouldn't be upset.

She knew she should stay out of it, but Michael and Ruby weren't making any progress. It was her job as his sister and one of Ruby's best friends to take on the role of matchmaker. What was that saying? It's easier to ask for forgiveness than to ask for permission. She would apologize for intervening later. Maybe while giving their wedding toast?

"Hello there," Bill said as walked into the house with Barbara.

"Dad? What are you doing here?" Melanie asked as she tried to stand but failed.

Ruby and Britney were by her side in no time to help her.

"Look at you! How many months are you?" Bill asked, avoiding the question.

"Does anyone know you're here?" Melanie asked.

"No, I wanted to surprise you kids. I thought you would all be happy," Bill said, getting upset.

"Michael and Tiffany are on their way over, and I don't think he'll be happy to see you here."

"He's still upset over that? I thought he would've moved on by now."

"Easier said than done," Melanie said under her breath.

"Come in, please," Ruby said as they greeted Bill and Barbara.

"Melanie, you are glowing," Barbara said sincerely, yet trying to lighten the mood.

"Thank you. I'm almost seven months pregnant."

"I can see that the twins are growing nicely."

"They sure are. I can't wait to meet them."

"Do you know the sex of the babies?"

"They are fraternal twins, one boy and one girl," Melanie answered with a huge smile on her. It always brought so much joy to her to talk about her kids.

"Where's little Ryder?" Bill asked as he looked around.

"Cade took him to the farmer's market. They should be home soon. I'm sure Ryder will be happy to see you both." Melanie replied.

"I hope you don't mind us intruding like this. I just really wanted to surprise you kids and spend some time together."

"It's no bother. I don't know how Michael will feel about your unannounced visit."

Unbeknownst to Melanie, Ruby had already texted Tiffany that Bill and Barbara had arrived at Melanie's house and were waiting for them to show up. Tiffany said she would relay the news to Michael and hopefully could keep him from turning the car back to Mary Elle's house.

Ruby gave Melanie's shoulder a small squeeze as a sign of reassurance that everything was ok. Cade had asked Ruby and the rest of the gang to keep Melanie's stress levels as low as possible during her pregnancy.

Suddenly, there was a soft knock on the door. Britney ran to open it, and there were Michael and Tiffany.

"Hello, everyone. Sorry, we are late," Tiffany said as she walked inside and greeted her father and stepmother.

"Hello kids, I'm so glad to see you both. I wanted to surprise you," Bill said, trying to gauge their moods.

"Hi, Dad," Michael muttered.

"Son, it's so great to see you. I was hoping we could all sit down and just talk. Well, there are many things I wanted to say," Bill began as he took a seat on the sofa.

"Would you both like something to drink?" Melanie asked as Ruby placed chips and dip on the coffee table.

"Yes, please," Barbara answered.

"I know things have been difficult for us all. I know I'm the one to blame. All my indiscretions have surfaced and hurt you, including your mother and Barbara. I would like to say I'm sorry for not being the father you all needed and for not being around for your basketball games, father-daughter dances, field trips, birthdays, summer vacations, and even graduation. I can't make up for all that time that has been lost, but I realize that life is unpredictable, and we don't know how much time we have left and what's important isn't a career or how much money we have in the bank accounts, or how many women we can get but what's important is family and loved one. All the blessings God has given me, I have taken for granted. I am here today asking for your forgiveness."

"Dad, I forgive you. I don't hold any grudges against you," Melanie said with sincerity.

"Dad, I know that you've always worked hard so that we can have everything we ever needed. I also understand that you're human and make mistakes. I forgive you for not being there for us like you mentioned, and I forgive you for cheating on mom. She didn't deserve it, but you had your reasons, I suppose. I hope that you truly realize the pain you caused her and somehow make amends," Tiffany replied in a polite yet stern tone.

"Michael, did you hear what I said?" Bill asked as he sat there with a stone face and in silence.

"Dad, I'm upset. You made me lie to mom about your affairs. It crushed my heart to know that you were with other women and would come home to her. I would see her crying in silence when you didn't show up as you had promised us you would. She tried hard to be strong for us and be there for us when we needed you. It's unfair to all of us, but as Tiffany said, you must have had your reasons. I choose to forgive you because I want to be rid of this hatred and move on," Michael said, meeting his father's eyes as he spoke.

"Michael, I'm sorry I placed such a burden on you. I now understand I did wrong, and I wasn't the male role model you needed. I know you are different from me and are a better man than I will ever be. I love you, son, and wish you learn from my mistakes."

There was a long pause. Things were awkward for Britney and Ruby, who had made their way to the kitchen to allow Bill to speak with his kids in private. They couldn't help but eavesdrop.

"Actually, I have something to say as well…" Barbara started.

"Honey, don't, it's ok," Bill said as he gave her hand a gentle squeeze.

"Bill is truly sorry for everything. I have seen him crying himself to sleep, regretting all the terrible decisions that he's made which have affected you all. I also wanted to apologize for my part in this whole mess. It all started as a game for me. Bill knows this. I just wanted to get back at Mary Elle because I hated her back then. I just wanted her to hurt. After losing my husband, I was very jealous of everything she had. I just wanted Mary Elle to feel a little pain, so I thought flirting with Bill would do the trick, but little did I know I would fall in love with him. He had other affairs that I knew about. I didn't care. I was one of them, and I wanted him to be mine, so I told him I would confess to Mary Elle about our affair unless he divorced her and he chose me. He said I didn't have to give him an ultimatum, that he loved me and wanted to be with me, so that's how the divorce came about. But what I didn't know what that Samantha was still trying to get him back, and that's when she realized he had left Mary Elle for me and this whole revenge plan came into motion. Michael, I'm sorry that you got caught up in our mess. I'm truly ashamed. I hope you all can find it in your hearts to forgive me," Barbara said.

The group fell silent, and no one knew what to say. Melanie looked two Michael and Tiffany, and they were both still trying to process Barbara's confession.

"I think that something we've all learned in the last couple of years is that we're all flawed individuals. Nobody in this room is perfect, but that makes us human. At the end of the day, we are a family, and we will get through this together," Melanie said, repeating words her mother had told her repeatedly. She'd never understood how true they were until this very moment.

"Melanie is right...I think it's time that we all forgive and move forward. We've been through a lot, and honestly, I don't think I can handle any more crazy revelations," Tiffany said with a laugh.

"Michael?" Bill said.

Everyone turned to Michael. He had been the quietest and was known for bottling everything inside. Michael swallowed, and his adam's apple bobbed in his throat.

"You're all right. It's time to forgive and move on. I've carried this burden on my shoulders for a long time, and I think I'm finally ready to move forward. I've held myself back for way too long," he said as he looked to the kitchen where Ruby and Britney were.

CHAPTER 16

Michael and Bill spent the next day fishing. They'd invited Bob along too as a buffer. So far, they hadn't had much luck, but they remained hopeful.

"Want one?" Bill asked, holding out a beer for Michael and Bob to see.

"I'll have one," Bob said.

"I'll take some water," Michael said.

He'd been trying to stay away from all the liquor.

Bill tossed him the water and joined them on the camping chairs they'd set up by the river.

"How are you enjoying living here?" Bill asked Bob.

"It's nice. Some days I miss going to work and being busy, but I prefer spending time with my beautiful bride."

Michael had always looked up at Bob and Rita. No matter what life threw at them, they always worked it out together. They were an authentic example of what a relationship should be like.

"Maybe Barbara and I should consider moving here..." Bill said.

No one said anything for a moment, and Bill laughed.

"You should see your faces," he said, pointing at them.

"I think everyone is better off having you at a distance," Bob said as he looked at Michael to back him up.

"Relax, I know no one wants me here permanently. It was just a joke."

"Michael, what's going on between you and Ruby? I heard she ended her engagement," Bob said, changing the subject.

"Yeah, she did. But nothing is going on between us. She hates me," Michael said as he stood to grab another water bottle from the cooler.

"Michael, you know I don't enjoy butting my head where it doesn't belong, but can I just say something?" Bob said, catching Michael by surprise.

"Sure," Michael said.

"I've seen you two playing this little game of cat and mouse for far too long. Be a man and get your woman. She will not wait around forever. You dodged a bullet when she ended her engagement. You don't want someone else to come around and take her from you."

"I don't think Ruby will ever forgive me."

"Don't be an idiot," Bill said, finally speaking up.

"No need to call people names," Bob said as he noticed Michael tensing up.

"You say you don't want to be like me. You think you don't deserve Ruby because you're too much like me? Isn't that it?" Bill asked, raising his voice.

"Yes, that's right," Michael answered.

"Well, the only way you'll ever be like me is if you act like an idiot and let that woman go. Own up to your mistakes and apologize to her. Do everything you can to win her back. Don't be like me. I wouldn't own up to anything, and I sure as hell wouldn't try to change for the better. You gave me a chance when you were a young boy to be better, Michael. You told me to come clean to your mother and stop having affairs, but I didn't listen. Now look at me, I've come so close to losing everyone that matters to me, and I still can't seem to get things right," Bill had gotten up and was pacing now as he shouted this at Michael. It was a Blackburn family trait to pace when you were upset. "Michael, you've always been a better man than I could ever be. Stop beating yourself up, son."

* * *

After a long night with the family, the girls pampered themselves by going to Winding Creek for a haircut and blow dry the next morning. While at the salon, they also got a manicure, pedicure, and facial. Not ready to go back home, they went to the gastropub next door to the salon.

"We look amazing," Tiffany said as they stood in front of the bathroom mirror at the gastropub.

"I wish I would've cut my hair too," Britney said as she ran her fingers through Melanie's slick A-line bob.

Melanie had chopped off her shoulder-length hair, claiming that with three kids, she wouldn't be able to keep up with it. Britney had only gotten a glaze and blowout. Tiffany had gone for long layers with side swept bangs, and Ruby had done a deep moisturizing treatment for her curly red hair and blown it out.

"Your hair looks great," Melanie told her.

"Let's take a selfie," Britney said as they gathered together for a photo.

"I've really missed you guys," Ruby said once they were done with the photo.

"We've missed you more," Tiffany said, hugging her.

"We really have," Melanie said, joining in on the hug.

"Hey, wait for me," Britney said as she too joined in.

The girls laughed and headed to their table to order their

appetizers and drinks, except for Melanie, who ordered a sweet tea. After they ate, they headed back to Melanie's house to continue their girl's day and to hang out.

"That's strange. Michael's car is here. I wonder if everything is ok?"

"I'm sure everything's ok," Tiffany said as she got out of the car and helped Melanie.

"Welcome back, ladies," Cade said as he took in Melanie's new haircut.

"Do you like it?"

"Yes, I do. My hot wife. I love it, actually," Cade said as he caressed her hair.

"Aw, thanks. I think it'll be easier for me to do my hair once the twins are born."

"Hey Michael, we didn't expect to see you. It's a pleasant surprise," Ruby said, trying not to blush.

"Actually, I'm here to see you," Michael said flat out.

"Well, here I am," Ruby said, trying not to be so awkward in front of everyone.

"Where's Ryder?" Tiffany asked.

"He's taking a nap. Today was an adventurous day for him. He tried some homemade jams with crackers," Cade said excitedly.

Cade loved Ryder and really enjoyed being a father to him. He has always expressed his desire to take him camping, hunting, fishing, and teach him woodwork, among other things. That had always been one thing that Melanie had prayed for in a husband after she had divorced Everett. She wanted Ryder to always feel loved and have a positive father figure in his life. Cade, Melanie, and Tiffany went to the kitchen, leaving Ruby and Michael alone in the living room.

"Would you mind coming out on the deck with me?" Michael asked Ruby.

"I would love to," Ruby said as she followed Michael to the deck.

The sun was about to set, and Ruby noticed a small basket, flowers, and a blanket by the Adirondack chairs. She felt a small flutter in her heart, remembering how sweet Michael had always been while dating. He spoiled her with flowers, chocolates, and anything he saw that reminded him of her while they were apart. She still had all the gifts he'd gotten her because even though she hated him, she couldn't bear to part with them.

"You look beautiful," Michael said once they were seated.

"Last time I cut my hair like this, you said I had an afro," Ruby said.

That memory was fresh in her head. She'd been so excited to get a haircut with her mom at a fancy hair salon, and she couldn't wait to show the girls and Michael. When Michael had seen her, he'd been speechless, and she thought that meant he liked it. Instead, he asked her what she'd done to her hair and said it looked like she had an afro.

Michael broke out in laughter, now sitting next to her as he, too, recalled the memory.

"I can't believe you're laughing!" Ruby said with a pout.

"I was a dumb boy. I said that because that was the moment I realized how much I liked you," Michael said.

"So, instead of saying something nice, you bullied me?" Ruby asked incredulously.

"As I said, I was a dumb boy. I should've said that your hair looked great, and I'd never seen anyone more beautiful."

Ruby felt her cheeks starting to heat up. Her pale complexion was betraying her again.

She cleared her throat and said, "So, you said you wanted to talk?"

"Right, of course. Ruby, I owe you an apology and an explanation..." Michael said as he turned his seat to face her.

"I'm listening..."

"Peter Miller never stood you up. I told him to say that because I wanted to take you to the dance myself."

"Why didn't you ask me then?"

"I don't know. Also, I told Kyle Jeffries to leave you alone after I found him kissing Christy Evans during an away game. I told him I'd beat him up if he didn't."

Ruby remembered her high school boyfriend Kyle Jeffries dumping her unexpectedly. She'd never known this was the reason why.

"I think I've known that I was in love with you since the first time my sisters made us pretend to get married in our backyard when I was nine years old..." Michael said, trailing off.

"Michael... why didn't you ever tell me?" Ruby asked.

"I thought I didn't deserve you. I still don't think that I do, but I can promise you I will spend the rest of my life trying to be the very best man for you."

"Michael," Ruby continued, "I don't know what to say. You've known how I've felt for you all these years. I have also felt like I wasn't enough for you. I've seen the girls that always flirted with you, and they were all so beautiful, and I'm just a plain Jane."

"You're not just a plain Jane. You are beautiful, smart, funny, hardworking, honest, modest, caring, and kind, and I dated those girls just to get attention. I was just pretending they meant nothing to me. Samantha could never compare to you. That has been my biggest mistake. I'm truly sorry for the way I ended things and for hurting you. I don't know how else to show you. I regret it all. I'm sorry," Michael said, as his voice broke a little.

"Michael, I forgive you. I don't want to lose your friendship. You mean so much to me. I could never just walk away from you. I have to confess that I was lying to myself as well.

I went on a blind date and met Axl. I knew I didn't love him as I do for you, but I kept telling myself that it was ok as long as I didn't feel so alone. When you broke up with me, it left a huge gap in my life. I not only lost my boyfriend but my best friend as well. It was lonely. That's the only reason I accepted to be in a relationship with him and then he was ready to settle down, and he proposed, and I said yes without even thinking. I didn't want to hurt him, either. It was all just a big mess. I also wanted you to know that I was better off without you, that I had found someone that cared for me and loved and wanted to spend the rest of his life with me. I thought maybe you'd see I wasn't a loser or just a plain Jane, but someone that deserved to be loved and that I was special," Ruby unloaded onto Michael.

"I did not know how much pain I caused you. I'm sorry. I know my words aren't enough. I know you might not trust me or even consider being with me again, but this is the absolute truth: I love you," Michael said as he reached for her hand and kissed it.

* * *

EVERYONE INSIDE MELANIE'S house was peering out the window, trying to listen to what was being said between Michael and Ruby, but the sun was setting, and the crickets had started making their sounds. Even an owl decided to start hooting early.

"Can you guys hear anything he's saying to her?" Melanie asked them.

"No, but I see she's blushing and smiling," Tiffany answered.

"Ladies, give them some privacy. I'm sure Ruby will dish out all the details when she comes inside," Cade said in an annoyed tone.

"He's right. Let's just wait to see what she tells us," Britney said as she went to sit in the living room.

Tiffany and Melanie looked at each other and shrugged their shoulders. They were not moving from this spot until they knew there was a happy ending involved.

* * *

RITA WAS in the back storage area when she heard the door chime.

"Hello, and welcome," Rita said as she entered the boutique from the storage area to greet the customer that had just arrived.

"Rita, it's me, David."

"Oh, hi David, nice to see you. How are you?" Rita said as she poked her head from behind the boxes, she was carrying.

"I'm doing very well. How are you?" David said as he came around the counter and took the boxes from her.

"I'm fine, just putting some supplies away in the storage. How can I help you?"

"Well, I need to place a special order with you."

"Oh, I see," Rita said with a huge smile on her face. She thought she knew what kind of order he wanted to place but would not jump to any conclusions.

"I'm thinking about proposing to Tiffany, and I know she's always said she doesn't like diamonds. She's always loved your designs and the opals you use on your jewelry. Could you please help me design a unique engagement ring for her?" David asked, smiling and hoping that Rita would agree.

"Of course, I would be honored. Lucky for you, I know her size and just what she likes."

"I'm so excited. I know this is going to be the ring that she would love and cherish. I also wanted to ask what ideas you might have for the actual proposal," David asked with a concerned look on his face.

He wanted everything to be unique yet something that would define them as a couple.

"Well, I guess we have our work cut out for us," Rita said, smiling.

CHAPTER 17

"We're all getting ready to head out for Dean's grand opening at the Farmers Market. Are you coming with us?" Mary Elle asked Thomas.

"No, but you all have fun," Thomas said, not looking up from the fishing reel he had taken apart.

"Are you sure?" Mary Elle asked.

She didn't want him to miss this moment. She knew Thomas would regret it once he wasn't upset anymore.

"I'm sure," Thomas said, not looking up to meet her gaze.

"It'll be at the farmer's market on the square if you decide to come..." Mary Elle said as she grabbed her purse and headed out the door.

The farmer's market was buzzing, and it didn't take long for Mary Elle to find Dean's food truck. It was very bright, and there was already a line forming outside. David and Jasper had bought a red ribbon for him to cut before officially opening. Mary Elle wished Thomas was here to see this.

"Mom! Over here," Tiffany said, waving at Mary Elle from a canopy across the food truck.

"Shouldn't we be making the line?" Mary Elle asked as she watched more people get in line.

"No, Dean said to sit here, and we would be the first he serves," Melanie said as she fanned herself. It was a beautiful summer day at Willow Heights.

There was a heat wave going on, and if Melanie's pregnancies were anything like Mary Elle's, she knew they didn't do well in the heat.

"How are you feeling?" Mary Elle asked her.

"I'm starving like always," Melanie said with a laugh.

Michael and Ruby arrived hand in hand, and when they noticed everyone watching, they pulled apart, and Ruby's cheeks turned bright red.

"I hope I'm not late," Thomas said as he joined them.

"You came!" Mary Elle said, jumping out of her seat to greet him with a hug.

"I couldn't miss this. I knew I would beat myself up if I didn't come," Thomas said.

Mary Elle kissed his cheek, and the group by the food truck hooted and hollered because Dean had just made an appearance. Dean surveyed the crowd, and when his eyes landed on Thomas, he motioned for him to join him. Thomas made his way to Dean, and they exchanged a warm embrace. David handed a very large gardening sheer to Dean to cut the red ribbon. Mary Elle giggled, trust the boys not to be able to find a proper scissor.

"Thank you all for coming here today," Dean said as everyone pulled out their phones to photograph and record this moment.

"Thomas, I called you up front here today because I know that this food truck wouldn't be possible without you. You took me in when I was just a naïve boy that thought he knew it all. You helped me become the Chef that I am today, and I can never thank you enough," Dean said as his voice cracked.

Thomas wiped a tear from his face and hugged Dean again, and told him how proud he was of him.

"Everyone else here, thank you. Thank you for supporting me and for sharing the word about my truck. None of this would be possible without you as well," Dean said as he cut the ribbon.

Dean had prepared some platters for Thomas and the Willow Acres crew, which he served before returning to the food truck to take orders from the hungry customers.

The event was a huge success. Dean also had a lot of new customers following his blog and social media account, where he shared short videos of himself cooking easy recipes. Even Patty showed up to show her support.

"Hi, Ruby," Melanie said and wiggled her brows.

"Hi, Mel…" Ruby said.

"So, anything new with you?" Melanie asked, leaning in close, trying to get Ruby to spill the beans on what's going with the hand holding.

"Not much," Ruby replied, not giving anything away.

After Ruby and Michael had their small picnic in Melanie's backyard, they didn't really share much information. They just announced that they were working on their friendship and had made amends, which everyone was delighted to hear, but no juicy details about what was actually said were provided by Ruby. The girls respected Ruby's decision and decided not to press her or Michael. They figured they needed to straighten things out before announcing anything formally. Melanie felt joy when she saw them arrive at the Farmers' Market together, holding hands. She knew they had figured something out already.

"I see. Well, I'm happy to see you and Michael are happier now. I don't judge or condemn your decision to date or not date. I love you both very much and just want to see you both happy," Melanie said as she gave Ruby's hand a small squeeze.

"Thank you," Ruby said, smiling and blushing.

Cade had been in line with Ryder at Dean's food truck. He wanted to support Dean on his first day and place an order like a loyal supporter. He had ordered all-American sliders with loaded French fries and creamy lemonades.

"That looks delicious," Melanie said as Cade and Ryder walked over with the food and drinks. Ryder was now a toddler; he was helping Cade carry the lemonades.

"Thanks, buddy," Cade told him as Ryder placed the lemonades on the table. He did it with so much care.

"Let's dig in," Melanie said.

Tiffany and David moved closer to join them. Ruby and Michael were a little awkward, trying to avoid being too close in front of them.

"It's silly. Just come and sit next to us. Don't pretend you aren't dating," Tiffany blurted out as she took a bit of the chill hot dog that came with Dean's platter.

"Tiffany..." Ruby said, gasping and wide-eyed.

"It's ok. We will admit it. We are dating," Michael said, trying to calm Ruby down and smiling. He secretly wanted everyone to know the good news.

"Well, there you have it. It is official," Cade announced loudly for their group to hear. Mary Elle and Thomas looked up and smiled, Bailey and Molly as smiled and cheered them on. Everyone was happy for them.

DeeAnn, Paul, and Gregory arrived late but joined their tables and enjoyed Dean's delicious food. Gregory loved spending time with Mary Elle and DeeAnn. It brought back memories of their mother and gave him joy. He loved sharing his stories about their parents, war, and everything in-between.

Rita and Bob sat next to Mary Elle and Thomas after ordering from Dean's food truck.

"Rita margarita. Tell me about Emma," Mary Elle said as Rita and Bob set their food down.

"She wrote me a letter before I moved to Willow Heights, and I guess it had gotten lost in transit. It finally arrived, and I called her up, and we briefly spoke over the phone, and she asked if she could visit us, so now, I'm planning activities while she's here. I've called the kids, and they got super excited, so they'll be coming over and staying at our house. Alexander and Caroline are bringing the baby. I didn't want to tell Emma she's a grandmother over the phone, and I think it's best if Alexander tells her himself."

"Incredible. I'm just blown away. God is truly great. He answered another one of our prayers, Rita. I'm so happy for you. Not only is she coming to visit, but she's sobered up and trying to get her back on track. That's commendable. I can't wait to see her when she comes to town."

"I think she would like everyone to have dinner at least once while visiting here. Who knows, maybe she falls in love with Willow Heights and moves here," Rita said with a hopeful smile.

"I heard even Bill joked about moving to Willow Heights. Can you imagine that?"

"Nope, I can't," Rita said, shaking her head and laughing.

"Bill met with the kids, and they finally hatched it all out. I'm so happy they are maturing and learning to forgive and let the negative things go. Keeping things in doesn't help them heal."

"I totally agree. I can see that it helped them. Even Ruby and Michael look like they are on good terms now. Those kids, it's like we all knew they loved each other before they realized it themselves," Rita said, smiling as she looked over at their table.

"Isn't that the truth?" Mary Elle said, laughing.

"Even Bob could see it, and he's clueless, right Bobby?" Rita said teasingly.

"Uh, yes, darling," Bob said, not sure what he was agreeing with.

"Oh, Bob, these gorgeous ladies have us so smitten we don't even care what they say about us; we just go along with it," Thomas said as he patted Bob on the back, causing the men to laugh.

"Aren't we lucky to have these stud muffins?" Mary Elle chimed in.

"We sure are," Rita said as she looked at Bob. He was the love of life.

They have been together through thick and thin, even when people thought they would not last, since they started dating at such a young age. They proved everyone wrong. They are still in love with each other as if it were the very first day. Rita still gets flustered when Bob compliments her, and he's the same way when Rita walks into any room. It's as if he had been in darkness until her presence was there with him, then there's light.

* * *

SIENNA WAS WALKING around the farmer's market, looking for tropical fruits for her daily smoothies, when she caught sight of Jamal. Jamal was Dr. Banks' brother, a pediatrician who had just moved to Willow Heights to help Dr. Banks' clinic grow. They worked together, and Sienna had a crush on him since the day they first met. Sienna, trying not to be too obvious, tried to casually look at the fruits and not stare at him.

"Hi Sienna," Jamal said as he waved at her.

"Hi, nice to see you out of the office," Sienna said as she waved back, hoping she wasn't acting weird.

"Those pineapples look great," Jamal said as he walked to the fruit booth, she was at and held a pineapple to his nose and sniffed it.

Sienna wasn't too sure what he was doing. She decided to just smile.

"This one is good, ripe, and it smells delicious," Jamal said, holding it out to her for a quick sniff.

"You are right. It smells delicious. I'm doing smoothies and fruit salads as a healthier snack option."

"That's great. I love fruits. I'm not too keen on vegetables. I don't know if I've told you, but I spent a year of practice down in Jamaica. Fruit abounds there, and everything is so natural, tastes so good."

"I didn't know that; it sounds like paradise."

"Yeah, I guess you could say it was a kind of paradise. It was a slower-paced environment, and the beaches were absolutely gorgeous."

"Has Shandra been to Jamaica?"

"Not recently, but she has been. Her husband, Leroy, is Jamaican, and let me tell you, he can cook some delicious food."

"So much I didn't know about your family and you," Sienna said, trying not to blush.

"I recommend you add a little turmeric to your smoothies. It helps reduce inflammation, vitamin D for an energy boost, and magnesium to help with stress."

"Thanks; I was researching healthy smoothies that would help me with stress. I love my life and job, but sometimes, it's draining."

"I know, I completely understand. I learned about natural remedies while I was in Jamaica. It never hurts to try natural medicine as well. I like to combine both with my patients."

"Yes, I've noticed. I thought that was very interesting."

"Well, I have to get going. My girlfriend is flying in today.

She's a nurse and was finally able to take some time off to come to visit me. I hope you will meet her while she's visiting."

"I would like that," Sienna said, knowing she didn't sound cheerful.

"Have a great rest of your day," Jamal said as he waved bye and walked away.

Sienna felt like a ton of bricks had just fallen on top of her. She was crushed.

"What's wrong, Sienna?" Tiffany asked as she saw the gloomy look on Sienna's face when she returned to the group.

"Oh, it's nothing."

"Come on, you can tell me. I thought we were friends?"

"It's just that I ran into Jamal, and we talked for a minute, and everything was going great..."

"But what happened then?"

"He said he was expecting his girlfriend to visit him. She's arriving tomorrow, and he wants me to meet her," Sienna said, sounding like she was holding herself back from crying.

"I'm sorry to hear that, but it doesn't mean you can't be friends and get to him better."

"That's true. Thanks."

"No problem, and who knows, maybe he introduces you to one of his friends, and you end up dating that guy instead?"

Sienna smiled and shook off the sadness. She hadn't been lucky in romantic relationships and men, but she was always hopeful she would find her prince charming one day.

* * *

BRITNEY WAS ENJOYING BEING BACK with everyone again. She never knew how much she missed this small town until she returned. It was the same way every time.

"Hey guys, sorry I'm late. I had trouble getting out of the house today," Jasper said as he reached the area where the rest of the Willow Acres crew was still sitting enjoying their day off, chatting and having Dean's delicious offerings.

"Jasper..." Britney said softly. It wasn't like her to be weak in the knees over a guy.

"Britney, I didn't know you were in town," Jasper said as he sat across from her.

"Yeah, I came for a two-week visit. Sorry, I didn't let you know..." Britney said, unsure how to say she's sorry for not texting or calling him back.

Jasper smiled at her and didn't seem to hold any resentment toward her.

"It's ok; I know a big city girl like you must be super busy. I'm glad you are visiting and hope you have a great time," Jasper said as he stood up to give her a sweet kiss on her cheek, which she wasn't expecting.

Jasper was truly different from any other guy she had ever dated or befriended. He genuinely cared for her and accepted her just the way she was. She knew she was a flimsy friend and needed to work on that, and his reaction caused her to make that promise to herself.

"I hope we can spend some time together as well," Britney said as he sat back down across from her.

"I would really like that. I have missed you, Miss Brit-Brit," Jasper said, smiling.

Britney felt like the burden she didn't realize she was carrying was suddenly lifted from her. She understood Jasper meant much more to her than she knew. She didn't want to ruin their friendship, so she had to work to be a true friend and be there for him as well. Britney would not take him for granted anymore.

EPILOGUE

Emma had finally arrived to visit Rita and the family in Willow Heights. She had to cancel several times because things kept coming up that prevented her from going, but the day was finally here.

"Emma!" Rita said as she ran outside when she noticed the car coming up their driveway.

Emma got off the car and ran to greet her sister. They hugged for what seemed like forever and couldn't stop looking into each other faces as they wiped the tears from each other's cheeks.

"I can't believe I finally made it!" Emma said as she saw her kids standing around them.

"Mom, it's really you," Amanda said as she, too, cried and joined them in their embrace.

"Alexander, Andrew, my boys," Emma said as she pulled them into the hug.

Everyone was so emotional, and the moment was captured by Caroline, who had been video recording on her cellphone, and Bob, who had taken out his old trusty camera to take photos.

"Let's go inside so we can talk and share what we have all been up to," Rita said as they walked inside her home, where Sienna and Penny were waiting anxiously to greet their auntie, Emma.

"Emma, this is your niece, Sienna," Rita said as she watched her sister's face full of shock.

"No way! Oh, my goodness, she's so beautiful," Emma said as she walked over to meet Sienna and gave her an enormous hug.

"And this is Caroline, your daughter-in-law, and Ren, your grandson," Alexander said as Caroline offered the baby.

"Oh, my goodness, I'm speechless," Emma said as she greeted Caroline and her grandson, Ren.

"Nice to meet you, Emma," Caroline said as she handed the baby to Emma to hold.

"I don't know what to say," Emma said while taking it all in.

"It's ok, mom. We are happy you found your way back to us and that we have finally reconnected," Alexander said as he hugged his siblings.

There was a knock on the door, and Bob said he would get it.

"It's probably Mary Elle and the kids," Rita said.

"Oh good," Emma said as she sat up in expectation.

Bob walked back into the room with an older man and a young lady behind him.

Sienna stood up and asked, "What are you doing here?"

"We wanted to surprise you," the woman said.

"Who are all these people?" the man asked.

"Olivia, dad… this is my family…." Sienna said.

"Family?" the woman asked as she looked at Rita and Bob.

Bob was now standing next to Rita with his arms around her.

"They are my biological parents," Sienna clarified.

"Oh my goodness, we had no idea," the man said.

He came up to Rita and introduced himself as the man that had raised Sienna.

"My wife would've done anything to be here today," he said.

"You're not upset?" Sienna asked.

"No, of course not. We always believed this day would come."

"Everyone… this is my dad and my sister Olivia," Sienna said to everyone else in the room.

At that moment, Mary Elle and the rest of the family walked into the room.

"The family keeps getting bigger," Mary Elle said.

* * *

THANK you for reading Reconnecting in Willow Heights. I hope you enjoyed it! The next book in the series is A Christmas Wish in Willow Heights. Click here if you'd like to join Mary Elle and the rest of the gang in the next book. The first book in the Winding Creek series can be found here.

LET'S BE FRIENDS!

Join Abigail's Newsletter for reminders of upcoming releases.

JOIN ABIGAIL'S Reader Group for: First Looks, exclusive giveaways, and more!

Manufactured by Amazon.ca
Bolton, ON

35679210R00070